You're surprised at all the blood.

He looks over at you, eyes wide, mouth dropping open, his face almost as white as his shirt.

He's surprised, too.

There's not a lot of broken glass, though, just some tiny slivers around his feet and one big piece busted into sharp peaks like a spiking line graph, the blood washing down it like rain on a windshield.

He doesn't say anything clever or funny, doesn't quote Shakespeare, he just screams. But no one can hear him, and it would be too late if they could.

CHARLES BENOIT

YOU

HARPER TEEN
An Imprint of HarperCollinsPublishers

HarperTeen is an imprint of HarperCollins Publishers.

You
Copyright © 2010 by Charles Benoit
All rights reserved. Printed in the United States of America.
No part of this book may be used or reproduced in any manner
whatsoever without written permission except in the case of brief
quotations embodied in critical articles and reviews. For information
address HarperCollins Children's Books, a division of HarperCollins
Publishers, 10 East 53rd Street, New York, NY 10022.
www.epicreads.com

Library of Congress Cataloging-in-Publication Data
Benoit, Charles.
    You / Charles Benoit.— 1st ed.
        p.   cm.
    Summary: Fifteen-year-old Kyle discovers the shattering
ramifications of the decisions he makes, and does not make, about
school, the girl he likes, and his future.
    ISBN 978-0-06-194706-3
    [1. Choice—Fiction.   2. Conduct of life—Fiction.   3. High
schools—Fiction.   4. Schools—Fiction.]   I. Title.
PZ7.B4445You   2010   2009043990
[Fic]—dc22   CIP
                                                            AC

Typography by Joel Tippie
12 13 14 15 16 CG/RRDH 10 9 8 7 6 5 4 3 2 1
❖
First paperback edition, 2012

To you. You know who you are.

YOU

You're surprised at all the blood.

He looks over at you, eyes wide, mouth dropping open, his face almost as white as his shirt.

He's surprised, too.

There's not a lot of broken glass, though, just some tiny slivers around his feet and one big piece busted into sharp peaks like a spiking line graph, the blood washing down it like rain on a windshield.

He doesn't say anything clever or funny, doesn't quote Shakespeare, he just screams. But no one can hear him, and it would be too late if they could.

You're thinking, this wasn't the way it was supposed to go, this shouldn't be happening. And now things are only going to get worse.

You're just a kid.

It can't be your fault.

But then there's all that blood.

So, maybe it is your fault, but that doesn't make things any better.

And it doesn't matter one way or the other.

Think.

When did it go wrong?

The break-in?

No, before that.

The party?

That was part of it, but that wasn't when it started.

Zack?

Of course, yeah, it would be easy to say it was Zack. But that's not it, is it?

Before Zack.

Before Ryan. Before Max or Derrick or that whole thing with the wallet.

Before Ashley.

Before tenth grade even began.

You run your finger down the list of homeroom assignments until you spot your name.

Kyle Chase—room 202—Mr. Lynn.

You're looking through the other names when Max comes up behind you, pretending to bump into you as if he didn't see you, like he always does.

You ignore him. Like you always do. Max is the closest thing you have to a best friend in this school, and that pretty much says it all, doesn't it? Back in eighth grade you never said two words to him, but that was before everybody you hung with went to Odyssey High. Things are different now.

"See who's in your homeroom?"

Of course you see who's there. You walked halfway around the building to check the list, but you act as if you don't hear him.

"*Ashley.*" He leans in as he says it, his voice getting all nasal like he's five frickin' years old.

"So?" You shrug, wondering for the thousandth time why you ever told him anything.

"What do you mean, *so?*" He's getting loud now and you just wish he'd shut the hell up. He'd be all right if he wasn't so immature or deliberately stupid, but that's pretty much everything he is. When he's not around anybody, when it's just you two, he's different. Not a lot, but enough. You ignore his question. He's used to it.

"I got Lynn," you tell him, and he nods. Mr. Lynn is the whacked-out English teacher who likes poetry way too much, but he's always been fair to you and to the other so-called hoodies, the name coming from the black sweatshirt jackets you wear. The rest of your schedule might suck, but at least homeroom will be tolerable.

"I got Perez," Max says. "Derrick's in there, too."

You nod, but you're thinking about Ashley Bianchi, something you've been doing since June, when she left for her family's cottage up on some lake. You tell yourself that summer would have been a lot better if she had been around, positive that you would have actually called her up and gone out to the movies or something. And there would have been times when her parents were out or your parents were out and you could have been together without everybody standing around staring. But before you can think too much about it, about this hookup that would

have been excellent, two chimes sound and teachers step into the hall to corral everybody into their
homerooms.

Welcome to the official start of tenth grade.

Welcome to the last year of your life.

Mr. Lynn reads off the attendance list and you
raise one finger when he calls your name. He smiles
at you and says "Welcome," just like he did for the
lacrosse players and the honor-roll students and you
wonder why the other teachers can't treat you like
that.

The room's dead quiet. After months of sleeping
in till noon, six o'clock came too early and everyone has that glazed-over, already-bored look in their
eyes. You recognize most of the people in the room,
know about half of their names, but there are some
kids who are obviously new, doing their best to look

like they've been here before. *She's* sitting up front on the other side of the room, and when Lynn calls your name she turns in her chair, a look on her face like she's surprised to see you, and she smiles and waves. You can't help but smile back and you give a goofy wave and immediately feel like an idiot. She has that effect on you.

She's got a dark tan, helped along by her Italian genes, and like every other white girl in the class, in the school, in the country, she's wearing her hair long and straight and parted on the side. You remember her hair being longer at the end of the year but then realize that she must have gotten it cut for the start of school, probably the same weekend she bought the jeans and shirt she is wearing. You know every outfit she wore in ninth grade. This one is definitely new.

Last weekend you were supposed to get a haircut too, but you told your parents that you forgot. And you didn't buy any new clothes, either. You've got drawers full of black T-shirts and worn-in jeans, and there are three hoodies in your closet, two regular black ones and a black one with these flaming skulls on the arm that your one cool aunt bought you last Christmas. Your friends drill on the sheeplike posers in their Aberzombie & Fitch sweaters and Aéropostale button-downs. You never bother mentioning the T-shirt/ jeans/hoodie uniform you all wear.

Lynn's reading off the day's schedule. He tells the class things they already know, like how the school has a rotating schedule and that today you'll spend a short time in all of your classes and that lunch will be blah blah blah and tryouts for blah blah blah will be after school in the auditorium and right then, ten minutes into your first day back to school, you start counting how many days it will be till the end of the year so you can get back to what you did over the summer.

Which was nothing.

But it wasn't this.

Math.

It's your favorite subject. Which surprises you.

Last year your teacher tried to convince you that you had a real "aptitude" for math, but all you got in the end was a B minus. The truth is you weren't even trying. But then you got low Cs and Ds in all your other classes and you weren't trying there, either, so maybe you are good at math after all.

You like it because either you're right or you're wrong. Not like social studies and definitely not like English, where you always have to *explain your answers* and *support your opinions*. With math it's right or it's wrong and you're done with it. But even that's changing, with Ms. Ortman up there at the whiteboard saying how this year you'll be writing something she calls Mental Notes, which *explain* how you solved the problem and *support* your answer, saying that having the right answer isn't as important as explaining how you got it and bam, just like that, you hate math.

"Now, tomorrow you'll have a quiz worth sixty percent of your grade this quarter." She pauses like she's some stand-up comedian before she adds, "Only kidding," as if it wasn't obvious. But then you notice half of your classmates sitting there with their eyes all popped out and you think, are they really that stupid?

She glances up at the clock, so of course everybody else does, and she sees she's got eight minutes left in the shortened period. Time to launch into the math version of the same speech you've heard in all of your classes so far and you wonder if they teach this time-wasting crap at teacher school.

"The first day of the year is always my favorite," she starts, and you already know where this is going. "All of you begin with an A plus, nobody has turned in their homework late, I haven't had to send any of you to the principal or give you detention or call your parents." She nods in your direction. "I always think of the year as a big, blank canvas. Everything you do throughout the year is like a brushstroke, and how you fill in your canvas is completely up to you. Some of you have your year all sketched out. Soccer in the fall, then into rehearsals for the winter concert, then it's tryouts for either the basketball team or the school musical—unless of course you're like AJ here, and you do *both*." And as if on cue, the class looks at handsome, athletic, all-sport AJ with his perfect smile and his J.Crew polo shirt, and he fakes an embarrassed shrug and does this little wave thing like he's saying "aw, shucks," and you find yourself hoping some fat defensive tackle takes out his knees in practice.

"It's important to keep in mind that you have control over your year," Ms. Ortman is saying. "If you don't like the direction your life is going"—and now you're positive she's looking at you—"then you have the power to change it. If you're not happy where you're at, figure out where you want to be and make it happen."

Which all sounds good, but you know it's ridiculous. You know where you want to be and there's no way you can make it happen.

Because if you could make it happen, if you could suddenly be back in eighth grade, you'd do it.

Because this time it'd be different. You'd work your ass off in all of your classes, just like Rick and Dan and Denica and Ari, and you wouldn't have spent all that time morphed to your Xbox, and when it came to picking a high school, you would have had the grades to go to Odyssey and not ended up at Midlands High. You'd be in the honors program with the friends you knew since fourth grade, doing those geeky after-school programs like MindQuest and Brainstormers and Forensics, which doesn't have anything to do with dead bodies. And you wouldn't have that scar on the back of your right hand and you'd be able to bend your middle finger all the way and you wouldn't have had to talk to counselors. And you wouldn't have to talk with losers like Max or Ryan or Derrick, either. You wouldn't have even *met* them.

But that would mean you wouldn't have met Ashley. And now you have to think the whole thing over.

One way or another, it's going to be an interesting year.

And then nothing happens until October.

Well, nothing worth mentioning. Every day you get up, go to school, fake your way through your classes, come home, get hounded about your homework, go online, fake your way through your homework, go to bed—and the next day you get to do it all over again. Weekends you hang out with the other hoodies, stay out as late as you can, sleep in as late as they let you, get hounded about finding a job, go to the mall, hang out. Repeat. Some of your friends get dragged to church, but other than your baptism—which you don't remember—and your grandmother's funeral—which you don't want to remember—you've never been inside a church. Weeks of your life have slipped by, as if that matters.

If there was something that all that time had in common, what your English teacher would call a "theme," it would be this: Don't get caught.

Don't get caught copying homework, don't get caught going to certain websites, don't get caught climbing up onto the roof of the mall at night, don't get caught stealing beers from the fridge in the neighbor's garage, don't get caught kicking the side of your father's Bronco, don't get caught slipping into all eight movies at the Cineplex, don't get caught sneaking glances at Ashley every chance you get or sliding up against her at lunch or finding yet another reason to put your arm around her shoulders. And definitely don't get caught lying wide awake in bed thinking about her.

You don't get caught, which means they must not be trying too hard.

Maybe it would have been better if you had.

But you didn't.

Saturday night. Halloween is this Tuesday and that sucks. You haven't gone trick-or-treating in years but there's something wrong about Halloween being in the middle of the week. No one's talked about it, but everyone's treating tonight as Halloween. Everyone's a little edgier, a little more pumped up. Not your parents, of course—they don't notice these things. Neither does your kid sister, but she's only five. Paige is excited about Halloween and she doesn't care what day it falls on. She's going as some Disney princess and she'll look real cute, which is good since she'll haul in more candy than she could ever eat. But that's what older brothers are for.

You're cutting down Thornapple Crescent to Ryan's house when you see Derrick cutting through the Fullers' yard and out to the sidewalk. He sees you and nods.

"What's up?" He says it all ghetto, like it's one word with a *z* in it, the way you all say it, just with a harder edge, like he owns it. Derrick's father's an accountant and his mother teaches French at the community college. It's hard to be ghetto when you live in a middle-class suburban development twelve miles from any building over four stories. But since he's black, people seem to expect it, so he gives it to them. You heard he's smart enough to have gone to Odyssey High but chose to come to Midlands. If it's true then he's not that smart after all.

"Goin' to Ryan's?"

"Yeah," he says. "Nothing else to do."

"Thought you'd be over at Shannon's."

He shrugs but doesn't explain. "Why ain't you with Ashley?"

"I didn't call her," and you're thinking, what the hell, does everybody know your business?

"I don't know what you're waiting for."

Neither do you, but you don't say it.

"Wanna call her now? You can text her from my phone. She won't ignore a message from *me*." He makes like he's digging in his coat pocket and before you can say anything Max comes running up behind you, bumping into both of you. He's out of breath like he's just run a mile, but you don't think that's ever happened. He's just a few pounds heavier than you, but he's the laziest person you know.

"Can't go to Ryan's," he gets out between pants. "His mom's going out. Won't let us over. Meet him at the park. He just called me."

You rattle off the expected swearwords, Derrick adds a few extra with Max rearranging the combinations. When did swearing become so easy? You still would never swear in front of your parents or most adults, but when you're with your friends it's like every fifth word. Why couldn't learning Spanish be that easy?

"It's gonna be cold tonight," Derrick says. He's got the same thing on as you do: jeans, a T-shirt, a sweatshirt, and a hoodie. It's what Max has on and what you know Ryan will be wearing. At least you'll all be suffering equally.

"We can go to the woods, start a fire."

"What, and smell like smoke for a week? No thanks." You pull the zipper on your hoodie up an inch.

It takes ten minutes to walk to the park. Ryan is sitting on top of one of the picnic tables. You can see the red glow of his cigarette twenty yards away. He's the only one you hang with who smokes and it's like he has to pick up the slack for the rest of you, burning through a pack a night, one cigarette right after the other. His mom smokes, so she can't smell it on him, but your parents don't and you try not to get too close to him so they don't start asking questions. As you walk over he reaches into a plastic bag by his side.

"Trick or treat," he says, and tosses you a can of Odenbach beer.

Derrick catches his beer with one hand. "Excellent. Where'd you get these?"

"Guy down the street. Helped him cover his pool. I noticed he had an outdoor bar. I found a whole six-pack in there and a bottle of tonic water."

Max opens his beer and takes a swallow. "Four of us, six beers. Big frickin' deal."

"Be thankful you get any," you say, hoping Ryan will give you one of the extra beers. You've never had more than three in one night and you're not all that crazy about the taste, but if you drink them fast enough you can catch a buzz.

Ryan flicks his cigarette butt toward the baseball diamond, the red dot arcing through the brisk night air, falling short of its target. "Let's get out of the wind." And with that you all follow him toward the back wall of Neil Armstrong Middle School.

It's a long and low building that your parents said was new when they went there. When you started sixth grade, construction crews were finishing up a major renovation and all the teachers could talk about that year was how *multipurpose* the building was and how lucky you all were to have such an *inspiring new learning environment*. But you had never been in the building before, so it didn't mean anything to you. Maybe that's when it started, when they told you how the new school would change everything you thought about school, it would be an *exciting adventure* and learning would be *fun*. And then it turned out to be just like any other school. So, yeah, maybe that's when it started.

. You kept up your grades that year—made honor roll every quarter—but you started to wonder, is this it, just more worksheets and quizzes and ridiculous group projects that wouldn't have challenged your kid sister?

That was the year you had to read the book about a kid in the Civil War, the book the teacher never stopped raving about, the one she called *truly inspiring*. But you couldn't get past the second chapter. That had never happened before. You used to love to read and always had a book in your hand. Then they assigned you the *truly inspiring* book and you found out how much reading could suck. So you read the back cover and you went online and then you wrote the book report. It was total BS and you knew it and you were actually nervous all weekend knowing that on Monday the teacher would "want to see you after class" or call your parents and let them know that you "were slipping a bit." And on Monday you got the book report back and there was a big old A plus on the cover.

If that wasn't the moment it was probably close to it.

Neil Armstrong Middle School. One small misstep for you, one giant waste of time for everybody.

Back against the wall, Ryan lights up another cigarette.

"I really hate American beer."

You all nod but none of you, not even Ryan, knows the difference. Then you start talking about other things that you don't know anything about, like which girls in your class are easy and what bands are coming to town and which teachers hate you the most and who's sleeping with who and which jocks are the biggest assholes, and then it happens. Max tugs on the back door, the one that leads to the maintenance room and the cafeteria, and it opens.

He looks over at you and his eyes are bugging out of his head and his mouth is hanging open and for a second none of you do anything. Then Max lets go and the door starts to swing shut.

If you had let it go, let the door close with a clear double click, would things have turned out differently?

Probably not, but you'll never know, will you?

You hold out your half-empty beer can, catching the door before it shuts.

"What are you doing?" Max says, his voice up an octave. "There's an alarm. The cops'll be here. We'll get busted. Take it out." He reaches for the beer can and you knock his hand out of the way.

"I don't hear any alarm."

They all tilt their heads and listen. No one is breathing.

"Maybe it's a *silent* alarm," Derrick says, "at the police station or something."

Ryan takes a long draw on his cigarette. "Let's find out." He looks at you. "Leave it there."

You nod and without another word the four of you dart across the grassy field, jump over the low chain-link fence and duck into the bushes that separate the school from the dark professional building where your dentist has an office. Your black clothes blend into the night and you can feel this hot rush of adrenaline just under your skin. For the first ten minutes every nerve is dancing and you take it all in—the bird that's sitting up in the tree by the bus loop, the slight breeze that rattles the hooks on the flagpole lines. You can smell Ryan's cigarette and the beer Max spilled as he fell over the fence. You're waiting for sirens or flashing lights or the cutting beam of a car-mounted searchlight, but nothing happens. If the cops do come they'll be too busy with the door and you'll be long gone before they even think to look for you. Then you remember the beer can and for a few panicked moments you think about fingerprints, but the more you think about it the less you worry—the cop would just pull the can out and shut the door. It's not like somebody died.

That's still weeks away.

You're sitting there in the cold and it goes from intense to boring real fast. After fifteen minutes you find yourself wishing the cops did show up, just so you'd have something to do.

Ryan is the first to stand. "All right, let's go."

You jump over the fence, Ryan and Derrick following after you, Max hangs back.

"The cops could still be coming." It's Max and he's right, and you all know it, but you keep walking to the sliver of light. There's a pause and then you can hear him stumbling back over the fence to join you.

You start off with big, quick strides, but you slow up as you get closer, easing your way into the light that fans out of the crack. Derrick goes around and grabs hold of the door handle and you catch the now-empty beer can before it falls to the concrete step. One hand on the door, Ryan leans in and looks around. "Hello," he says, repeating it, louder this time, and you all listen, expecting a reply, expecting a shouted hey-you-kids-what-the-hell-are-you-doing. But there's nothing, so you step inside.

Later that night, when you're lying in bed, looking up at a ceiling you can't see, you think about that door.

It was locked, just not pulled all the way shut, and that's why Max could open it. Not that it made a difference—there was nothing in the room anyway. Some empty plastic garbage cans, a couple wet mops, broken-down cardboard boxes. It smelled like stale milk in there. The double doors that led to the cafeteria were still locked and not even Ryan wanted to bust them open. Two minutes after you went in, you were back out, the lock clicking this time. A small distraction on an otherwise dull Saturday night.

But going through the door changed things.

Hanging out in the cemetery or over at that construction site where they were putting up the new track homes? Or that time you all lifted Derrick up on your shoulders and he pulled down that fire-escape ladder and you all ran around on the roof of Sears until you saw the cop car way over at the other entrance? That was trespassing. If the cops had caught you then they could have taken you to the police substation, the one next to the library and the town hall, and your parents would have had to come and pick you up and you would have been grounded and all that crap.

They *could* have done that *if* they had caught you.

Now *would* they have taken you in?

Probably not.

And would they have even caught you?

Hardly.

But this was different. It was trespassing, sure, but it was more than that. And while *technically* you didn't have to break in when you entered, you've seen enough cop shows to know that's the way it would have read on the police report, Breaking & Entering.

You're lying there safe in your own house, in the bed you've had since you were twelve, and it dawns on you what would have happened if you'd been caught. And all of a sudden your stomach flips over and you're cold and you start shaking and you feel guilty and ashamed and scared all at the same time and you think you're going to puke.

But you don't. The feeling passes, and what two hours ago was the most criminal thing you had ever done seems suddenly insignificant.

Another line crossed. And you didn't even notice.

Ten minutes later you're asleep.

Mr. Nagle asked you to stick around a moment after the bell.

"I'll admit, you have been working harder in class, and when you've done the lab work it's always been very good, and I haven't had to speak to you about not paying attention in quite a while. But . . ."

There's always a *but*.

It's a magical word. You can say anything you want, go on for as long as you want, and then all you have to do is add the magic word and instantly everything you said is erased, turned meaningless, just like that.

You're a really nice guy. . . .

Your mother thinks you need a new computer. . . .

You've been working harder in class. . . .

But.

You keep looking at Mr. Nagle as he explains how a few zero homework grades really knock down your average. You nod, and you're thinking that everything he is saying is true.

You *are* smarter than this.

You *could* be getting all As.

You *could* be on the High Honor Roll.

And that if you don't straighten up soon, you *won't* get into college.

You *won't* be able to find a decent job.

You *won't* amount to anything.

And you *know* it's all true.

But.

"So I go, 'I was gonna apply for that job,' and she's like, 'Well, you should have,' and I go, 'I'm the one that told you about it,' and she goes, 'Oh well,' like it's not her problem, right?"

You nod your head. You've got no clue what she's going on about, but it's Ashley, and you'd listen to her read the phone book if you could sit this close to her. You're sitting on the curb, waiting for the late bus, Ashley because she was getting help in math, you because you had detention. There're some other kids over by the benches and a couple of guys kicking a Hacky Sack—which you didn't think anybody did anymore—and it's surprisingly warm out and sunny and you're sitting next to Ashley, listening to her talk about nothing and you're pretty sure that this right here is the highlight of your year so far.

You met last year when you were both in the same science class, and almost every week you were lab partners. She liked working with you because you knew most of the stuff already anyway and you always got the labs done on time. Back in seventh grade you were in science club and you met after school to do experiments, sometimes even on the weekends. But you didn't tell her that. And she liked working with you because you weren't hitting on her all the time like the other guys in the class, mostly tenth graders who were repeating ninth-grade science. And she liked the cologne you wore, which was this after-shave your dad had given you last Christmas, as if you needed to start shaving.

And you liked working with Ashley because what guy wouldn't want to work with Ashley? Your friends called her cute but said she was kinda small in the boob department. You called your friends idiots and said they were kinda small everywhere. No you didn't. You didn't say anything. The less you got them noticing how hot she was, the better chance you had.

It started with science class, then sometimes you'd sit with her at lunch, not just you two but as part of a group. She didn't really hang out with the hoodies or the jocks or the drama club, just kinda floated around from clique to clique. She got along with everybody, and at Midlands that was a hell of an accomplishment.

"So I'm sitting there, doing my worksheet like he said, and he comes up and goes, 'Miss Bianchi, what do you think you're doing?' And I'm like, *hello*, I'm doing *your* stupid work, so I go, 'I'm doing the worksheet,' and he goes—"

Her eyes are not really blue but not green, either. Hazel? And she wears too much eye shadow, sort of a sandy-brown smear on her eyelids. But it's good being close enough to look into her eyes.

Why is it different with her? Other girls, you had

no problem with. With them you talked a couple times, texted a few nights, then made out somewhere. No big deal. But it's different now, with Ashley. You've never wanted to kiss somebody more, never wanted to do more, do it all, but you hold back. She's not like other girls, the kind you fool around with for something to do. You tell yourself that the right time is coming—soon—that you'll tell her how you feel. Maybe not tell her, just show her instead, you don't know yet.

But for right now, for this moment, it's good between you two.

Here are the Top Ten things that your parents say to you:

- Is that all you're going to do all day, sit in front of that computer?
- When I was your age I had two jobs.

- Why don't you wear some clothes that fit for a change?

- Turn it down. I can hear it all the way over here.

- You're not eating that for dinner.

- Did you do your homework?

- Stop mumbling and speak up.

- *Now* what did you do?

- Because I said so.

- No.

The second chime is still ringing and you're already out the door. Although Mr. Jansen finds it thrilling, the elastic clause of the U.S. Constitution fails to interest you or any other student in the class. You doubt that Mr. Jansen finds it all that interesting either, just part of that act every teacher puts on, trying to convince you that *this is vital to your future success.* Last week, when you were actually doing homework, you asked your father about the three-fifths compromise in the Constitution and he said he was never good at math. He had to have sat through the same classes, learned the same crap, which makes you wonder if the only reason they make you learn it is because *they* had to learn it.

It's not that classes are hard. Most of the time they're ridiculously easy. The textbooks are dumbed down to the point where your kid sister could probably read them, and the teachers go over and over and over the same stuff anyway, drilling it into your head so that they can ask you one hundred multiple-choice questions to get it all back out of you again. The teachers complain that the students today are all lazy, ignorant, and stupid. But the truth is that you're smarter than they are. You're not even old enough to drive and you already know that none of this matters. Not the English or the social studies or the math or the science. If it did, if it *really* mattered, they'd teach it in a way that made you want to learn it. But no, they've got to teach it in the most mind-numbing way possible, moving on without any real discussion to get to the next thing that's going to be on the test—the *standardized* test. Then when you take that *standardized* test they stand there in front of the class and actually tell you, "These tests are to help rate the school and won't affect your grade." And then they're *shocked* by the results.

And they say that the students are stupid?

So you go down the back hall, past the science labs, past the upper-level math classes, to the stairwell that will bring you out twenty feet from Ashley's locker, which is right across from her next class. It's geographically the farthest point away from your English class and if you talk with her for even two minutes you will be late and you will get detention. But Ashley will probably be staying after school and if she does you'll get the chance to wait for the late bus with her. Detention, you decide, may be the best thing that will happen to you today.

You push open the stairwell door and start up, two steps at a time. You're at the first landing when you see it, off over near the wall.

You don't carry a wallet. You *have* one, the one your grandmother gave you, but when she died you took everything out of it and put it in your top dresser drawer. It was getting worn out and you wanted it to last. You have that older one, the one with Velcro and a red Power Ranger on it, so it will never be used again. You wad up the few dollars you carry and stuff it with your school ID in your jeans pocket. It's not like you have a license or credit cards to worry about. But obviously somebody does, because sitting there near the wall is a black tri-fold leather wallet.

You look around first before you bend over to pick it up. You don't know why you look around, it's not like you stole it or anything, but you look around.

Maybe it's instinct, some caveman in your deep past learning the hard way to look around before he picked up some other caveman's coconut.

The leather's worn smooth and at the corners the black dye has rubbed thin. It's heavier than any wallet you've ever carried. You flip it open and there are at least ten plastic cards in the little pockets, all lined up so you just see a quarter inch at the top of each one. That's enough to identify most of them at a glance. A driver's license, a Visa card, a Starbucks card, a school ID, another bank card. And in that long slit pocket, two twenties, a five, and a bunch of ones.

There's a second—that's it, a second—when you want to stick the wallet in your pocket and walk away about fifty bucks richer. But that's not you. Later, they'll say that you did things like that—and worse—all the time. But you didn't. And later it won't matter anyway.

With your thumb you slide up the ID. The word

SENIOR is stamped across the photo like it was a major achievement only attained by the chosen few and not something everybody gets if they hang around long enough. You recognize the guy in the picture, some muscle-headed stereotype, but you don't know his name and there's no way he knows yours. He's a senior and a jock. You're a sophomore and a hoodie. In his world you don't even exist. Until now.

"Excuse me, I believe you have my wallet."

Okay, that's not what he says, not even close to what he says, but that's what he'll tell the principal he said, and the principal will nod as if this fine young man wouldn't say anything harsher than "golly," and only that if he were provoked.

But everybody heard what he said. That's what brought the crowd to the stairwell. That and the chance to see some underclassman get the piss beat out of him by a varsity lacrosse player.

You try to tell him that you just found the wallet

in the stairwell and that you were going to take it to the main office and that you're not a thief and you don't need his stupid money, but it's kind of hard to talk when someone's got a fistful of your collar rammed up against your throat. He's shouting at you, chin down, looking up under his eyebrows, the veins along his temples popping out. He spits when he yells and you can feel the spray on your face. You bring a hand up to pull his fist away, but he gives a jerk that catches you on the chin and snaps your mouth shut. Later, Max and Derrick will tell you what you should have done.

"You should have kicked him in the nuts," Max will say, kicking out an imaginary attacker in case you didn't understand.

"I would have popped that punk upside the head," Derrick will say in his best homie voice.

What they won't say, but what you all know, is that you couldn't have done a thing. He has sixty pounds on you and at least eight inches, and thousands of hours in the gym. He all but picked you up when he grabbed you, and when he walks you backward and slams you into the wall so your head bounces forward, your feet hardly touch the floor. He twists his hand a quarter turn and now you can't breathe, your collar tightening around you like a noose. You're holding the wallet out and you can feel your face turning red, but it has nothing to do with being embarrassed. You'll have plenty of time for that later. He brings his left hand up and rips the wallet from your grip, then backhands you hard on your ear. You're gasping now and your head's ringing and you watch as your hands try to claw his balled-up fist away, and then there's a couple of male teachers there pulling him off you. Suddenly you can breathe again and right away you lunge for him, swinging a wide punch that glances off a teacher's shoulder, the other swing, the big one, missing everybody, throwing you off balance, and you stumble forward. The one teacher grabs you now and pins your arms to your sides. He's old and bald and surprisingly strong.

The red roar in your head recedes and you can hear all of the students in the stairwell. Some are stuck in that "fight, fight, fight" refrain, others are doing the "what happened?" drill, and others, mostly girls, are laughing. The senior is taller and bigger than either of the teachers, but he lets them keep him from getting to you.

"He stole my wallet." He waves the wallet as he shouts like he's daring you to reach for it again, unable to control your thieving urges.

"I didn't steal it. It was on the floor," you say, and there's this strange crack in your voice. But nobody really heard it since everybody's shouting now and there are more teachers herding everyone out of the stairwell. The jock's still going on about how you stole his wallet, but the teacher's telling him to be quiet and the teacher that has you—Mr. Harris—lets go of your arms but stands close enough to let you know you shouldn't try to run. Not that you would, but if you did you sure as hell could outrun him.

They march you down the stairs and through the hall to the principal's office and of course everybody's gotta come out of their rooms and stare. You expect the students to do it—you'd do it—but there's half the teachers, watching you go past with that sour *now what?* look on their faces.

"I said that's enough. Knock it off." It's Mr. Coriddi, the other teacher, and he's talking to the jock and he's not kidding. He probably had to get up off his ass in the teachers' lounge to deal with this and then there's probably going to be some paperwork he'll have to fill out. He teaches twelfth-grade math. He doesn't like his job and he doesn't care who knows it. You can hear it in his voice. He sounds a lot like your dad.

Coriddi is walking fast—got a card game waiting, no doubt—and the jock's up there with him, walking that swagger that guys like him always walk. You and Mr. Harris are falling a few steps behind and he's breathing through his nose, but it's loud and there's a whistle to it. It's kinda funny, but you're not ready to let go of that pissed feeling yet. You had Mr. Harris for study hall. There were forty kids in the class and it was only for the first quarter of last year. You didn't think he'd remember you, but then he says, "Kyle, what class are you supposed to be in now?"

"English. Ms. Casey."

He nods. You don't know why he'd want to know, but you're glad he asked. Up ahead, Coriddi walks past the school's massive trophy case and up to the main office. He pushes open the glass door and points to a row of cafeteria chairs along the wall under a framed flag that you were told once flew over the White House. There's a long counter in the main office, and the receptionist and the secretary and one of the counselors who was looking up some files all turn to watch you come in. The jock sits down at one end, you take the other. He keeps flipping through his wallet, making sure that everything is still there, going back, flipping through again, just in case you reached over and grabbed something when he wasn't looking.

Coriddi leans against the counter. "Dave in?"

"I'll give him a call," the secretary says, and picks up a walkie-talkie off her desk.

The counselor looks over at the jock and rolls the file cabinet drawer shut. *"Jake?"* He says it like he can't believe what he's seeing, like the jock had three heads or something. *"Jake Burke?"*

"Hey, Mr. Linton," the jock grunts.

"Jake, what are *you* doing here?"

Seeing Jake in the principal's office is apparently news. Seeing Kyle Chase is not. The jock turns his head to look at you, then looks back at the counselor. "Somebody stole my wallet."

Coriddi snaps his finger and points at the jock. "No talking."

"He asked me a question," Jake says, and now his

voice is going up like he's looking for a fight and you're sitting there wondering how cool it would be if those two went at it right there in the main office. Running that thought through your head keeps you from punching the wall.

It takes ten minutes for the principal to arrive, two minutes for Coriddi to explain how he got it all under control, and two seconds for Mr. Harris to agree. The principal is checking with the secretary to see if he has any appointments coming up when one of the gym teachers comes through the office doors. He's tall and trim, with the kind of square jaw football quarterbacks always have. He's wearing track pants and a black and gold Midlands High Cougars sweatshirt. He's balancing a cup of coffee on the back of a green clipboard. He jerks his right-angle chin at Jake the Jock. "What are you here for?"

Jake's got his head tilted down and he's lost all that swagger. "Hey, Coach."

"Why are you here?"

Jake looks up to make sure Coriddi is gone. "*Somebody* stole my wallet and I had to get it back."

The coach looks at you. "You take his wallet?"

"No. I—"

"He's lying, Coach," Jake says, and he gives this laugh.

The coach keeps his eyes on you. "Did you take his wallet?"

"I found it in the stairwell. I was going to bring it to the office, but I didn't even get out of the stairwell before he was all up in my face."

"Gentlemen," the principal says, "I'd like to see the both of you in my office."

Jake jumps up first. You sigh and stand, glancing at the coach as you walk by. He looks you in the eyes and you're startled at what you see.

He believes you.

You've never had him as a gym teacher, you're not on one of his teams, you've never spoken to him before. But there in his eyes, something that says he believes you.

Well now, that was unexpected.

Everything else that happens—the accusations, the suspension, getting grounded—goes pretty much the way you thought it would.

HOW YOU GOT THAT SCAR ON THE BACK OF YOUR HAND PART 1: THE OFFICIAL VERSION

DATE AND TIME OF INCIDENT: *March 17, 7:10 a.m.*

TYPE OF INCIDENT: *Personal Injury*

BUS #: *202, Route 1C*

DRIVER: *Bob Presutti*

STUDENT'S NAME: *Kyle Chase*

DESCRIBE THE INCIDENT: *Student slipped on wet floor*

and fell across the seat, putting his right hand through

the glass of the window, lacerating back of right hand

DISPATCHER NOTIFIED: [x] YES [ ] NO

POLICE/AMBULANCE ARRIVED: [x] YES [ ] NO

POLICE/AMBULANCE REPORT #: 0317-A-14616-010

HOSPITALIZED: [x] YES [ ] NO

CHARGES FILED: [ ] YES [x] NO

PARENTS NOTIFIED: [x] YES [ ] NO

REFERRED FOR DISCIPLINARY ACTION: [ ] YES [x] NO

ADDITIONAL NOTES: *Responding officer requests*

student speak with school psychologist

The fourth time you go ahead and hit SEND. Her phone rings way too soon.

"Hello?"

"Hey, Ashley, what's up?"

"Eric?"

Eric? "No, it's, uh, Kyle."

"Kyle? Oh my *god*, we were *just* talking about you. How are you?"

Just talking about you? With Eric? Who the hell is Eric? "All right, I guess. Just hanging out."

"I can't *believe* they gave you three days and they only gave Jake one night's detention. And that was for swearing. It sucks."

She knows the jock's name? "Yeah. It sucks."

"I was at my locker getting stuff for my class and all of a sudden I hear Jake swearing his head off. F this, F that . . ."

She never swears. Well, not *really* swears. You first noticed it a few months back when she was pissed at her parents for something and she still didn't swear. You wonder why, but you never asked her. It makes her more interesting, special.

". . . then like *everybody* rushes to the stairwell, and I'm so short I can't see a thing. All I heard was that a bunch of hoodies mugged Jake in the stair-well."

"Who told you *that*?"

"I don't know, that's just what I heard. Then at lunch, Sophie told me how you got caught lifting Jake's wallet—"

"*What?*"

"—and I'm like, Kyle? No way—"

"Thank you."

"—I mean Jake would just *crush* you—"

"I didn't try to take his wallet. I found it. It was there on the stairs. I picked it up and was checking to see whose it was and then he comes slamming into me like I stole it."

"But you got suspended."

"They couldn't prove that I took it and they couldn't prove that I didn't, so they gave me three days for starting a fight."

"So they just couldn't prove anything?"

"*I didn't take his wallet.*"

There's a pause. A long pause. "Okay. So you didn't take his wallet. Jeez."

"Why would you think that I would? I don't *steal* stuff."

"I don't know, it's just that's what everybody was saying." She pauses again. "But I should've known."

"Yeah, you should've known."

"It's not like you to do something like that, especially to somebody like *Jake*."

You know what she means, but you say, "What do you mean?"

She gives a laugh, and for the first time you don't like the sound of it. "If you're gonna steal from anybody—"

"*I didn't steal anything.*"

"I'm just saying, *if*. God, don't get so freaked. *If* you were—*if*, Kyle—you'd be smarter than to try to jump Jake."

This is the point where you're supposed to say "I could kick his ass" or words to that effect, but really, you *are* smarter than that.

"*Anyway*," she says, dragging every syllable out of

the word, changing her voice to let you know that she's dropping the subject, "remember that job I told you about, over at the piercing booth in the mall, the one Cici went for? The manager called me. I got an interview tomorrow."

You'd like to go to the mall and just happen to bump into her after her interview and ask her how it went and suggest you go to Starbucks or something, but of course you're grounded. She's going on about what she's going to wear and what she's going to say and how she can get a 20 percent discount and how it's so great because it's right at the mall and part of you wants to point out that she doesn't have the job yet and another part of you wants to find out who this Eric is. But one part—the part that wins—just wants to hear her talk. So other than the occasional yeahs and nos, you say nothing. It's not what you want, not what you were hoping for, but you can hear her voice and, for now anyway, it's good.

Tuesday. Your first day back and there's a quiz in your math class. Ms. Ortman isn't sure what to do with you. The way it works is she's supposed to have sent any work she assigned for you to the main office where they gather it all together and then your mom comes in and picks it up, but from the way she's acting—telling you how she was *sure* she had sent that packet to the office and that maybe it got lost there or something—you know she didn't send it down. That's okay, your mom never came by to pick it up anyway, mostly because you never told her she had to. But if you told her this time she'd wonder why you didn't tell her the last time and you'd have to make up some story, so it's just better for everybody this way.

Back to Ms. Ortman. It's her second year and she's still trying real hard to save the world, just like all the new teachers. But when it comes to the rules and the paperwork, the stuff the older teachers worry about, she fakes her way through and hopes no one notices. You all notice, but why would you say anything? She's almost apologizing now and decides that, since the rest of the class is taking a quiz and since she really has to walk you through this next unit after school because you're an idiot, she's going to give you a pass to the library, that way you can catch up on the work you missed in your other classes. You both say yes, that's a good idea, knowing there's no chance of that happening, and you're out the door, pass in hand.

The first thing you check is the time on the pass. It says 9:14. You could change it to 9:44, but you'd have to avoid getting stopped for half an hour and that's not likely. So you go to the library, taking the longest route that could still be believable.

You spend a lot of time in the library. You used to be a big reader, horror mostly, but also those fantasy novels about guys with swords and women in metal bikinis. Mangas were cool for a while, but then the one bookstore that carried them got picketed by a church group and now they only stock G-rated graphic novels Paige would find dull.

You go to the library twice a week to get out of study hall. Not that you do any work there, but you go and sit by the magazines. And every time you're there, the librarian looks over now and then to make sure you're not sleeping. But—surprise—you're reading. *Time, Newsweek, U.S. News & World Report.* The articles are short and some are interesting and all of them are more relevant than what you're doing in class. Last week in American History, you were the only one who knew who the president of India was. The teacher didn't even know. "I'll check on that and let you know if you're right." Next day, of course, he didn't say a thing about it.

So you walk into the library and there's a ninth-grade English class over by the magazines, supposedly doing research but mostly just screwing around. You do a quick check of the room. You don't see anybody you hang with, so you head to an empty table over by the science books, a part of the library nobody is likely to visit. On the way you grab a magazine off the rack—*Maclean's*—push out a chair with your foot and slump down, ready to kill forty-seven minutes.

You're two paragraphs into a story about the Canadian Army when you sense someone standing by the table. You look up.

What if you hadn't looked up? What if you'd just kept on reading, ignored him until he went away? Or what if when you saw him, you'd taken off, left him there to find someone else to kill time with? Or stood up and sucker punched him before he said a thing? All right, that wouldn't have happened, but it all seems so random, doesn't it?

You look up.

He's about your age, maybe a bit bigger than you. He's wearing a bright red shirt under a black sport coat—the kind your father would wear—top button open and no tie. The shirt's tucked into a pair of jeans that are not as baggy as the kind you wear. A dork by anybody's standards. He looks at you for a second, then smiles this strange smile.

"My name is Zack," he says, "and I'll be your waiter today. Would you like to hear the specials or should I just start you off with something from the bar?"

You look at him and you can feel yourself scowling. The last thing you need is some retarded kid hanging around. Except he doesn't look retarded. He's standing there, his thumbs hooked into the pockets of his jeans, shoulders relaxed, way too cool to be retarded.

So he must be queer.

You say as much under your breath, loud enough for him to hear, adding a few of the appropriate F-words.

He sighs and shakes his head. "Such a predictable first guess. Sorry, wrong answer. But it's still your turn." He reaches over and spins a chair around and sits down at the corner of your table. "Try 'Bizarre New Kid' for a hundred points."

You ignore him and think about moving, but you were here first. You flip the page in the magazine and act as if you're reading the ad.

"Let's see, Watson," he says, and now he's pretending to have a British accent. "Black T-shirt, black hooded sweatshirt, baggy black pants, fashionably unkempt hair, horned skull ring on one hand, fingernails bitten down to nubs, sullen piss-off expression . . . yes, quite obvious. At some schools they're called the Freaks, at others the Burnouts, at one school in the east they're referred to as the F-U tribe, as that is their traditional greeting." He leans in on the table as if to get a closer look at you. "Here at venerable Midlands High, I believe the species is known as the Hoodies."

Head down, you look over at him. You want to reach out and smack that smug smile off his face, but if you got in a fight your first day back, your parents would seriously kill you. You look down at the magazine and realize you were staring at an ad for Viagra. You flick the page so hard it rips.

"I know, I'm amazing, but you'll get used to it in time." He drops the accent, pauses long enough so that he knows you're listening, and says, "Trust me, I know you will. Mr. Kyle Chase."

Your head snaps up—it's instinct—and you look at him, trying to look hard, but you can't keep the surprise out of your eyes. He's got your attention now and he knows it. He flashes his eyebrows up and down several times, that same stupid smile on his face.

No, not a smile. A smirk.

"You *are* Kyle Chase, fifteen, of 122 Woodbine Lane, aren't you?"

You are, but you just look at him.

"Yes, I know all about you, Mr. Kyle Chase, fifteen, of 122 Woodbine Lane. Like how right now your best grade is a C minus in math, that last year you put your fist through a bus window, that you have accumulated an impressive eighteen days of detention since September, that you were in no less than four fights last year, all of which you started, and that you have just completed three days' suspension for stealing Jake Burke's wallet."

"I didn't steal his wallet. I found it on the stairwell and—"

"Yes, yes, yes, it was *all* in the report, Mr. Kyle Chase, all in the report."

You feel your head tilt to the side, your eyes narrowing.

"Picture it, Kyle," he says as he leans back in his chair, balancing easy on two legs, his hands conjuring up the scene. "New kid in the school, history of . . . *indiscretions*. The principal—here playing the role of the stern but understanding adult who wants to give this kid a fresh start—calls said child to his office for the reading of the riot act. In the midst of his soliloquy, an unnamed secretary intrudes, says that there's a matter only he can address, and suddenly the new kid finds himself alone in the principal's office with nothing to read but the folders on the desk."

"You read the stuff on the principal's desk?"

He holds his hand out as if he's presenting you to a crowd. "And your science teacher had the audacity to say you don't pay attention. Well done, young Chase, well done. By the way, if the weather holds up there's a fire drill tomorrow, fifth period."

Then he does something you don't expect. He reaches his arm out across the table to shake your hand, old-fashioned style, the way your father taught you to shake hands when you were five. "Zack McDade."

You keep your grip on the magazine and look at him. His smirk has shifted a bit, not so smart-assed, but still there's something about it that pisses you off. He raises his hand an inch or two, just in case you missed it, but you leave him hanging.

"*Tsk, tsk, tsk*. Such manners." He doesn't look mad

or hurt or embarrassed — if anything he looks amused, as if this was the response he'd expected from you.

Behind him, the library doors swing open and one of the security guards steps in. With a stretched-neck, squinty-eye pose, she scans the room. She gives the magazine area a long look, sweeps across the empty fiction area and then over to where you're sitting. Naturally, she heads right for you.

Zack stands up and straightens his jacket, pulling the cuffs of his red shirt out the ends of the sleeves. "A pleasure meeting you, Mr. Kyle Chase. Let's do this again sometime."

The security guard is at your table before you can say anything worth saying. An F-bomb with her walking up would get you a quick six days' detention. You say nothing and close the magazine, wondering what you're in trouble for now.

"There you are," she says in that I'm-so-tough voice she uses, but she's not talking to you. "Who told you you could leave like that?"

Zack keeps his smile. "Let him that would move the world first move himself."

You both look at him.

"Socrates? Father of philosophy?" Zack pauses encouragingly, but neither you nor the security guard says a word. He sighs. "This is going to be a *long* year."

"Let's go," the security guard says, snapping her fingers and reaching for her walkie-talkie as they start back across the library. "This is Unit Two— found our new kid."

Over the static squawk and hiss of the main office's reply, you hear Zack ask if she hates her parents for naming her Unit.

"So she goes, 'Do you have a résumé?' and I hand her the folder and she opens it up and reads for like a minute and says something like 'You don't have a lot of job experience, do you?' and I'm thinking, *duh*, I'm fifteen years old. . . ."

Ashley stayed after school for math help again. You stayed after because Ashley was staying after, but you didn't go for math help like you were supposed to, you just hung out, waiting for her. Not that she knew, but you did. It's cold outside, so you're standing in the alcove by the side door. There's no wind here and what little sun there is slants in and warms the red bricks of the walls. She's got on a winter coat and she looks like a little snow bunny. Cute and sexy at the same time, if that's even possible. You, of course, are freezing your ass off, your black hoodie no match for the mid-November weather.

"The first thing she asks me is if I know Cici DiGenarro, and I *want* to say 'Cici? Yeah, I know Cici, she's a little lying brat who tries to steal her friends' jobs,' but I just smile and I say that I know her from school. . . ."

You recall something about a job interview at the

mall—a shoe store?—and you think you recall something about Ashley's best friend, Cici, going for the same job, but you're not a hundred percent sure, so you keep your mouth shut and nod along. Part of you wants to steer the conversation around to this Eric guy, find out who he is, how she knows him. Part of you never wants to hear his name again. And another part of you, a part you hope isn't so obvious when she leans into you to stay warm, doesn't listen to you anyway.

"So she gets to the education part and she's like, 'Oooh, honor roll. Impressive,' and I can't tell if she's serious or just screwing with me, ya know?"

Screwing with me.

Damn.

You can picture it. Easy. Hell, you picture it all the time. And even right now, your nuts frozen solid, thinking about it makes you sweat.

"Then she sees I played softball last year and she starts telling me about this team she's on, all women in their twenties like her, as if I care, but I keep nodding and smile and I ask her what position she plays. . . ."

Did she say honor roll?

"For the references I put down this lady I used to babysit for, and Reverend Keyes from my church. Think I should have asked them first if it was okay?"

You shrug and say no. Softball?

"So she tells me about the job, like how I'd have to learn to do piercings and if I got sick when I saw blood . . ."

How much do you know about her? You think about her all the time and you can imagine what it'd be like to be with her, what it would feel like, what her hair would smell like, the things she'd say, the things she'd do. But you just found out she's on the honor roll. True, it's only Midlands, but still. And she plays sports. Nobody you hang with plays sports.

"And they only do ear piercings, which is cool cuz I don't want to be touching some guy's slimy tongue. . . ."

You want to know more about her. You want to know what she thinks, what she dreams about, what she wants to do when she gets out of school, what her favorite bands are, which *Saw* movie she thought was best, which classes she hates, the kind of things she likes to do, you know, sexwise.

". . . a *second* interview Wednesday after school, so I'm like, sure, but come on, it's just poking holes in earlobes. . . ."

You think about getting to know her, the hours you'll spend on the phone, texting all night, hanging out on the weekends or after school like now. You don't mind just talking. That'll lead to other stuff, sure, but talking, yeah, that's okay. With her it'd be different. You could tell her what you really felt and not be afraid she'd laugh, even if you weren't sure what you felt. But she'd help you figure it out, and you'd help her, too, it would be—

"Well," she says as she punches your chest, "I said, do you think I should?"

You don't have a clue what she's talking about. You take a deep breath. "It depends," you say after a long, thoughtful-looking pause. "Is that what you *really* want?"

It's the kind of question your mother throws at you all the time, the kind that's supposed to keep you talking but that you always answer with the same shrug.

She looks up at you and smiles. "You're right. I don't know. I really don't know, you know?"

You still don't know, but you smile and you give her a quick hug, and she starts talking again, but you're busy thinking about how cool it would be to really get to know her.

"I'm done yelling at you, Kyle. I'm done hounding you about things you should do. Do you understand what I'm saying? I'm done."

It's your mom, and you understand what she's saying. You understood her the first time she said it, two years ago, and you understood her every time she said it since. And, like all the other times, you really wish she meant it.

Life would be so much easier if they just left you alone, let you do what you wanted. You wouldn't cause them any grief, you'd take care of yourself and make your own food and get yourself where you needed to go. But no, she doesn't mean it and even as she's telling you that she's done lecturing at you about how you need to grow up and learn to be responsible, she's circling around and lecturing at you about how you need to grow up and learn to be responsible.

"You're going to be sixteen soon, Kyle. *Sixteen*. Do you know what that means?"

What *does* it mean? You can get a job, but you could've done that at fifteen with a waiver on your working permit. You could get your driver's license, but your father has made it clear that you can't even get your permit until you get a job and have five hundred bucks in the bank to cover the jump in his insurance premium. You can't vote until you're eighteen, not that you care, and you can't buy beer until you're twenty-one, something you're beginning to care more and more about. And you have to be seventeen to legally drop out of school. You're not going to, but it's nice to know you have options. You remember reading somewhere that in some state in the South you can get married at sixteen without your parents' permission, so there's always that.

"I never see you hanging around with Rick or Dan anymore. You were friends for years. You should give them a call."

So they can tell you all about how wonderful it is at Odyssey? So they can ask you questions about Midlands and then glance at each other with that look while you're answering, like you're confirming all the things they heard about the dump? So they can tell you how they're going into AP classes next year? So you can sit around and talk about the good old days, back before you were a loser? So you can feel even worse about yourself?

"Or that pretty black girl. You know. What was her name?"

Denica. You met her in sixth grade. Back then she used to catch a special bus to the high school every day just to take eleventh-grade math. She was smart and had this funny laugh and she always smelled like cocoa butter. She was the first girl you ever kissed and you remember that she wore bubblegum-flavored lip gloss. Your mom always calls her That Pretty Black Girl, as if that's all that mattered about her.

"She was nice."

Yes, she was.

"You should call her."

Ah, but you did call her, didn't you? Back in

ninth grade. You talked for twenty minutes. Then you heard her mom in the background ask her a question and she said, "some boy," and her mom asked another question and she said, "No, he goes to Midlands." The way she said it and the way her mom laughed when she heard it made you wish you could take the call back.

"And I wish you wouldn't slouch like that when I'm talking to you. Sit up straight, why don't you? Is that how you would sit in a job interview, all slouched over like that? And did you ever pick up an application from the grocery store like I asked? It seems like that HELP WANTED sign is up every other week. You could have had that job if you had gone over the first time I told you. And how many times have I told you that you have to write up a résumé? Why did I bother buying that program for the computer if you're not going to use it? I'm telling you, Kyle, I am done talking to you about these things."

You wish.

Naturally, that Zack kid is in your English class.

He's sitting two rows over, but there's nobody in the seat between you, so you have a clear view of him. He's wearing jeans and sneakers, new, but neither in what could be referred to as the adolescent fashion of the day.

And he's wearing a lime green sport coat.

It looks ridiculous, especially with the yellow shirt underneath, yet it fits so well that you realize that it's not something his father outgrew. He's kicked back, all slumped down, his legs stretched out, his feet crossed at the ankles way up under Megan's seat. He's got the front cover of *Romeo and Juliet* curled around to the back, the book propped up on the edge of his desk, and for some reason he's laughing.

Ms. Casey wants you all to read Act II, Scene 1 silently to yourselves while she takes attendance or does whatever she does with her grade book every day before class. Nobody really reads when she says this, since you all know she's going to go back and have you read it as a class anyway. But it's Zack's first day and he can be forgiven for doing what he was told. It's the laughing part that has everyone, even Ms. Casey, glancing over at him.

"It's Zack, right?" Ms. Casey says, looking at him then at the paper in her hand, so it's obvious that she knows that's his name.

He looks up from his book, his laugh dying to an open-mouth smile. "No, it's Zack *McDade*. Right's just my nature." He gives a little wave and goes back to reading, the chuckling laugh starting up with the first line.

Ms. Casey closes her eyes and sighs and for once you can relate. She pauses a half beat longer than usual and even the nerdy kids are peeking over to see what she'll do. "Zack, we're reading silently to ourselves, so that means no distracting—"

"Sorry. Can't be done."

"Excuse me?"

"No problem, apology accepted," he says, and keeps on reading.

A line crossed, her tone shifts. "Mr. McDade."

He looks up and now everybody is watching. "Yes?"

"We are reading silently to ourselves. Do you know what that means?"

He tilts the book down and looks up at the ceiling, one hand coming up to his chin, like he's pondering the question. "Well," he says, drawing the word out with a growl, "since we can't very well read silently to each other, I'm assuming—and this is just a guess, so jump in if I'm way off base here—that you want us to consume Act Two, Scene One without verbalizing the words or the content therein."

Ms. Casey gives him an icy stare.

"Well then," he continues, "it seems we have a problem."

Her stare drops a few more degrees.

"Ms. Casey, as much as I'd like to comply with

your quite reasonable request, it is scientifically impossible to read Act Two, Scene One of *Romeo and Juliet* without laughing. It simply cannot be done." He sits up and gets this excited look on his face, flipping a page back in the book, then holding up his hand to stop her interruption before it starts.

"Mercutio is talking about Romeo and says, ''twould anger him to raise a spirit in his mistress' circle, of some strange nature, letting it there stand till she had laid it and conjur'd it down.'" He looks up at Ms. Casey. "You want me to read jokes about virgins, erections, and hand jobs without laughing? It cannot be done."

You're in the last seat of the row and even from there you can see her eyes narrowing, her nostrils flaring out. If you can see it, so can he.

"And then there's line thirty-eight. I mean I'd expect it in, say, *The Naughty Stewardess*. But a class assignment? You *sure* you should be letting us read this porn, Ms. C.?"

So, like everybody else in the class, you look at the line—the open-arsed part is obvious, but what's a pop'rin pear? And even though they're laughing, you know your classmates don't have a clue. This is Midlands High, not Odyssey. Students here don't get Shakespeare. Ms. Casey has all but said it since passing out the book a very long week ago.

But apparently somebody does get Shakespeare. Or he knows how to pretend he does.

Either way, it makes no difference.

Without taking her eyes off Zack, Ms. Casey reaches for the pad of preprinted forms they use when they send someone down to the vice principal's office. You know the form well and you wonder if she'll check the Disruptive Behavior or the Insubordination box.

Either way, it makes no difference.

At the door, checked form in hand, Zack turns back to face the class. "'Parting is such sweet sorrow, that I shall say good night till it be morrow.'" But before he closes the door, he looks at you and gives a nod. You nod back.

Two minutes later, the class is back to normal, the students pretending to read silently to themselves and Ms. Casey pretending to care.

The weather holds and there's a fire drill during fifth period.

Thursday morning. Homeroom. A summary of the things Ashley says during your eight-minute conversation:

- She got the job at the ear-piercing place
- Cici also got a job there
- This is a good thing because Cici is her best friend

- Next week she'll be spending Thanksgiving at her grandparents' house
- She wants a new phone
- She saw the funniest video online
- No, she has never seen a porno online and thinks it's gross
- She texts too much
- She thinks she needs glasses
- She would rather have contacts
- She asks if you know the new kid in school named Zack
- Just because someone wears a sport coat doesn't make him gay
- He got kicked out of class for swearing at Ms. Casey
- This is what everyone is saying
- She didn't know that he was in your English class
- She thinks what he really said was funny
- She thinks he sounds cool

- No, she is not kidding
- She has a test in social studies first period
- She really should have studied

With forty-five seconds left in homeroom, she asks you to explain the elastic clause of the U.S. Constitution.

"You didn't think I'd forget about it, did you?"

It's Thursday afternoon. You're in the boys' locker room. You're wearing a pair of black gym shorts and socks—your T-shirt is balled up on the floor and you don't know what they did with your sneakers. They had come in fast—you didn't see a thing and you are sure no one else did either. So it'll be your word against theirs. Guess who'll win that one?

Three members of the school's varsity lacrosse team are gathered around the back corner where your gym locker is located, watching as the team's co-captain leans his thick forearm into your neck, pinning you up against a row of cold, metal doors, the dial of a Master lock digging into the back of your head.

And of course it's Jake the Jock doing the talking, the "it" being the ass-kicking he promised you last week.

Thanks to the school's rotating schedule, your last class was gym. The gym teacher held everybody till right before the bell, so no matter how fast you changed you would not have made the bus.

So you didn't rush.

You were going to stay after school anyway, maybe see Ashley. Bump into her all casual—oh, you're here, too?—talk about nothing until her mother picked her up. That may not be such a good idea now, since in a few seconds you'll have a broken nose and a swollen-shut eye. Not a look you think Ashley will find attractive.

The jocks are all wearing jeans and polo shirts, the type of shirts these kinds of jocks always wear, neat and tailored looking, with the short sleeves that cling to their biceps and the colors that show off their late-fall tans.

If you yelled, shouted for help, there's a good chance the gym teacher might hear you and bust this up, but you wouldn't do that, wouldn't call for help. Better to get the piss beat out of you than call for help. It'd only take a few weeks to recover from a beating. Yelling for help would scar you for life.

Besides, you can hardly breathe as it is with his arm crushing your windpipe.

This is where Jake is supposed to say something like, "I'll teach you to try to steal my wallet," or, "How'd you like a knuckle sandwich?" or some other stupid movie-line crap, but he doesn't, and you watch—everything slow motion now—as he rolls his lower lip between his teeth, clenches his fist tighter, draws in a sharp breath, and cocks his arm back an extra inch.

Then a voice.

"And . . . *cut*."

A voice you know.

"Thank you, gentlemen," Zack says, leaning over the top of the row of lockers behind Jake, a cell phone in his hands. "That's a wrap."

Everything hangs in place—the slack jaws of Jake's pals, Jake's fist a dozen inches from your face, the sweat rolling down your nose—as Zack jumps down the back of the lockers and strolls around to join the group. He's looking at his cell phone, his thumb texting away, the green plaid of his sport coat a few shades off from the color of the painted concrete walls.

And still nobody moves.

"Excellent. Outstanding. Each of you. Truly well done." Phone held in his fingertips, Zack claps softly. "Jake's brutish anger, the stoic defiance in young Chase's eyes. And you," he says, aiming his claps at the other jocks, "supporting roles are so difficult, yet you brought them to life. Bravos all around."

"What the hell you think—"

Zack points to his phone. "Have you seen these? They're amazing. Not the phone part, the video part. The resolution is *unbelievable*, even in low light like this." He glances up at the fluorescent lights then turns his attention back to his phone. "The zoom feature is very cool. You can get in *real* close. And the audio. That's probably the most impressive feature."

Jake jerks his forearm and your head bangs against the locker, and he turns to look at Zack. You can feel something warm running down the back of your neck, but you can breathe again.

"Hey!" Jake shouts. It's a voice that's used to being obeyed. "I'm talking to you, freak."

"Be with you in a second," Zack says, holding up a finger of his free hand, his thumb dancing across the keypad. "Just sending this off."

"It's that queer kid," one of the jocks says, finally

placing the face or the sport coat. The others agree and add in their own descriptors.

"Gentlemen. Such language. Besides, *I'm* not the one who spent the last twenty minutes lurking around the locker room waiting for some boy to get undressed."

Jake grunts and steps over the bench. "That's it. You're dead."

Zack is smiling that smirky smile and you think, yup, he's dead. Jake gets right up on him, bumping Zack with his chest and glaring at him, staring him down to the tile floor. Zack meets his eyes, the smile still on his face. "Jake, Jake, Jake. Aren't you even the slightest bit curious what I was doing?"

You see the edges of Jake's mouth twitch, but he keeps leaning in so that Zack has to bend back to keep their eyes locked.

"I filmed the whole thing, Jake. All of it. Starting out in the hallway when I heard you and your *compadres* talking about how you were going to beat up young Chase here, the sneaking around the locker room, the way you came around the corner, ambushing him as he's pulling his shirt over his head. The way you slammed him up against the locker was *quite* impressive. Oh, and gentlemen?" Zack allows himself a quick glance at the other jocks. "You're all in it, too. Unquestionably, undeniably you."

Jake inches back on his heels. "So? You show it to anybody and you're a dead man." Jake chuckles and his friends chuckle, too. But there's no mistaking the nervous edge.

"Won't you ever learn, Jake?" You watch as Zack taps the keys on his phone, holding it out as Jake's voice, tinny but clear in the phone's small speaker, repeats the threat. "Now I've already emailed the video to myself. Whether I email it to Principal Lyttle and Coach Comeau is completely up to you."

You're certain that Jake is not as dumb as he looks,

but he proves otherwise. "What do you mean?"

Now Zack leans forward and Jake steps back, playing it off by resting an elbow on the top of an open locker door. "If anything unfortunate should happen to either Mr. Chase or myself—for the rest of the year—I'll be sure to include you when I send out the video."

"Oh, like I'm supposed to be scared of—"

"Yes," Zack snaps, and for once the humor is missing from his voice. "And you are. Now go away before I decide to punch young Chase in the nose just to blame it on you."

Jake scowls for a moment, stands a little taller, but it's over and you all can feel it. He laughs like it's not the big deal it is and pushes past Zack, bumping him out of the way, his crew in tow. He rounds the corner and you hear a fist dent in a locker—you can relate to that—then a moment later the crash bar to the exit being kicked open.

You don't know what to say, so you rattle off a

dozen swearwords, then snatch up your T-shirt and throw it in your backpack. Zack is standing off to the side, pushing buttons on his phone. You should say something, so you start to mumble "thanks," but he cuts you off.

"I'd love to stay and chat, but I'm already a tad bit late for my appearance at the detention room. I'm sure you can take it from here." He smiles, does that wave thing, and is gone.

HOW YOU GOT THAT SCAR ON THE BACK OF YOUR HAND PART 2: WHAT YOU TOLD THE SCHOOL PSYCHOLOGIST

I don't know why everybody keeps saying that I'm angry all the time.

Okay, not *every*body.

My father, for one.

And I bet the bus driver, now.

But I'm not angry *all* the time.

Sometimes, sure.

Everybody is.

So why does everybody keep saying it's just me?

All right, not *every*body.

Jesus.

It's just an expression.

No, I'm not angry now.

But I could be if you want me to be.

I'm glad, too.

What really happened?

You read the report.

I slipped and fell into the seat and my hand went through the window.

I don't care if you don't believe it.

Why couldn't it have happened that way?

Well, maybe I fell in farther than I thought.

Maybe my arm was higher, I don't know.

Why should I tell you something different?

And get suspended?

Why do you care?

Right.

Okay, we'll play what-if.

What if I told you that I wanted to punch that kid in the face?

The kid that was sitting there.

I don't know, just some kid.

He pissed me off.

Something he said.

I don't remember.

All right, something about me being stupid.

Why would I care what he thought?

Because he pissed me off, okay?

Damn.

I said I don't remember.

I'm not getting mad.

He said something, so I went to hit him.

Professional help? Yeah, right.

Because I didn't hit anybody.

I could have, but I didn't.

I don't know, I just didn't.

Probably would have knocked him out.

But I didn't. Damn.

I hit the window instead.

No, that's not what happened.

We were playing what-if, remember?

I told you, I slipped.

There's nothing else to talk about.

Can I go now?

It's Friday night and you're hanging around outside the 7-Eleven, freezing your ass off. They only let you in the store one at a time and Max is in there buying a Slurpee. It's thirty degrees outside and he's buying a drink made with crushed ice. And he's taking forever about it, too, filling the cup's domed lid one minute squirt at a time.

Derrick was a no-show, but you figured that. He and Shannon had been fighting all day at school, something he said or didn't say or something else altogether, you didn't want to know. He was home, on the phone no doubt. Damage control. It would be different for you and Ashley. You'd never argue with her. You'd just agree with everything she said. You're sure she'd like that because that's pretty much what you do now.

Ryan is outside with you, leaning up against the spot where there used to be a pay phone. You don't remember there ever being a phone, but there had to have been one once because they still have that metal hood that says phone on the side. He's got Kristi pulled up tight against him, her legs snaked around his, both of them holding their cigarettes off to the side as they stick their tongues down each other's throats. There's a vinyl banner across the front of the building—OPEN 24/7. BECAUSE THIRST NEVER SLEEPS—and the way it's hanging it blocks the store's spotlight, putting the two of them in a shadow. But it's still light enough to see her grinding up against his leg like she does every time she gets near him. She's in the eleventh grade, and she and Ryan have been banging away every chance they get for the past year.

She's okay looking, you guess. She has mousy colored hair that's frayed at the edges and she wears too much makeup, even by Midlands' standards. Her voice sounds old, all gravelly and raw, and she swears more than any guy you know. Once last summer, when Ryan was visiting his dad, you two got busy in the shed in your backyard, your first time, her first time that week. After all the hype, you were surprised at how little it meant to you and disappointed that it meant even less to her.

You were in eighth grade when your parents gave you the Talk. Which was a little late, since in sixth grade you had written that report on ways to prevent sexually transmitted diseases. But they wanted to avoid any future "problems," saying that it was important that you "got it straight." You wanted to tell them that getting it straight wasn't the problem, but they seemed so serious that you didn't say a thing. And that made them more serious. In the end what they did try to explain you knew years ago, your mother wrapping it all up by saying, "Remember, Kyle, every girl is somebody's sister." You know what she meant, but she obviously didn't know Kristi. Besides, Kristi is an only child.

Max walks out of the store, Slurpee in hand, grinning, and you wonder if his parents did a lot of drugs before he was born. He holds up the cup. It's the size of a small mailbox. "I mixed the orange one and the Coke one and the energy drink one and the pineapple one all together."

"How's it taste?"

"Like crap. You see the guy in there?"

You look past him and at the manager behind the counter, a guy your father's age with even less hair and a nervous way of looking around, like any second he expects some crackhead to burst in with a shotgun. Not that it's likely, but working alone in a store like that, your mind probably wanders a lot. "Yeah?"

"See his coat?"

You look again. It's the bright red smock they wear with a name tag and a button that says WE ID EVERYONE. "Yeah?"

Max grins. "Maybe your freaky friend Zack can borrow it sometime."

You could tell him that he's wrong, that it's not a sport coat and that Zack isn't your friend, but that would just keep him going on about coats and smocks and everything, and it's just not worth the effort.

Kristi comes up for air and looks over at Max. "Oooh, a Slurpee. Can I have some?"

"Sure," Max says. What else could he say? The rule is any decent-looking girl asks to share your drink or have a lick of your ice cream or take a bite of a sandwich, you say yes. It's gross if you think about it, especially like now, Kristi's lips all covered with Ryan's spit, but there are some rules even you wouldn't break. She peels herself off Ryan and runs over to Max, her feet scuffing the sidewalk like a little kid. She does the up-and- down straw thing first, then takes a long sip. Ryan makes the expected jokes about better things to suck on and she replies with the expected suggestive comments, Max giggling like he hasn't heard them all a hundred times before, adding his expected third-wheel line so Ryan can make his well-rehearsed just-try-it-and-see-what-happens threat, and you're wondering when the last time any one of them had an original thought was. You're all standing there—Ryan still leaning in the ex–phone booth, Max and Kristi near the store entrance and you somewhere in between—when Jake the Jock pulls up in his car.

It's an electric blue Honda Prelude, new, with tricked-out rims and sidelights and on the backseat window a decal of that cartoon kid taking a piss. He's playing something loud and thumping and he gives the engine a rev before shutting it off and stepping out.

"Later," Max says, snatching his Slurpee from Kristi and bumping into both of you as he ducks around the corner of the building. Ryan leans deeper into his metal cave, telling Kristi to get her ass over there. You? You stand there. What else you gonna do? Run away? Hardly.

Jake pushes the car door shut and starts for the entrance. And that's when he sees you. He slows up a bit and you watch as his lips pull back, his teeth clenched. He angles toward you, not much but enough to put you within range. He's five feet away when his phone goes off, some college fight song for a ringtone.

"What up?" he says into the phone, staring you down as he walks past, letting you know he's blowing you off, as if you aren't worthy of anything more than a glance. And that's fine by you. He goes into the store, still talking on the phone, and you think now's a good time to leave. You stood your ground, no need to push it. You turn around and see Ryan and Kristi halfway down the block, Ryan's arm draped over her shoulder, his cigarette glowing like a nightlight.

You crack open the warm beer and take a seat on top of the picnic table. "You left me hanging back there."

Ryan shrugs and sits on the big rock that marks the far edge of the park. Max and Kristi are on the swings, their feet on the ground, rocking back and forth. Kristi isn't into beer and once you and Max leave, she'll break out a joint for her and Ryan. She isn't into sharing, either.

You say it again, hitting each word so Ryan knows you expect an answer.

"It's none of my business. What's between you and that asshole is between you and that asshole."

"So you would have let him beat me up?"

He shrugs again. "You could've taken him."

Wrong answer. You take a swig of your beer, part of the six-pack Max stole from home.

"Besides, if he would have swung, I would have been on him."

"From halfway down the street?"

He smirks and shakes his head. But it's a lame smirk, no confidence behind it, all bluff. "I was there. Max, where was I?"

Max looks up from the drag marks in the dirt. "I don't know. I had to pee, so I went back by the Dumpster."

You smile. "Really? Then they must have moved the Dumpster to the other store."

"Kyle, just get over it, okay?" Kristi says. "It's no big deal. It's not like he hit you or anything. He didn't even *notice* you, okay? Don't be such a wuss."

You stand up and toss an almost-full beer in the direction of the slide. "I'm not the one who walked away."

And then, for the first time, that's exactly what you do.

You walk in the door at eight o'clock. You haven't been home this early on a Friday night since the end of eighth grade. Your father looks at you, grunts something about homework, then goes back to watching a finger-jabbing commentator bully his guests, shouting over them and telling them to shut up. Your dad loves this guy. Big surprise there.

Your mom just put your sister to bed. You wonder if she still reads her stories the way she used to, the way she said she did with you. She walks into the kitchen as you're getting the milk out of the fridge and she stops, her eyes popping open, looking at you as if you just swam in from Australia. "Kyle, you're home early."

Your mother is a master of the obvious. Most of what she says to you is stuff you already know or stuff you'd have to be an idiot not to see.

Kyle, your room's a mess.

Kyle, you're failing science.

Kyle, you're old enough to have a job.

Kyle, you never bring any books home.

Kyle, at this rate you're not going to get into college.

Either she enjoys pointing out what you already know or she thinks you're an idiot.

"Kyle, that's a full gallon of milk. Hold on so you don't drop it."

She thinks you're an idiot.

"There's some doughnuts in the box on the counter," she says, pointing to the box on the counter that says DOUGHNUTS. "Your dad's in watching TV."

You grab a chocolate-glazed doughnut, your

favorite. "I'm gonna go up to my room."

She pulls out a chair at the kitchen table in front of a cup of tea. "Sit with me for a minute."

So you sit.

"How's everything going at school?"

You shrug as you pull the doughnut apart, dunking bits in the cold milk.

"Are we going to be getting any surprises when your report card arrives?"

"I don't think so," you say, and you're being honest since, if they've been reading all the notes your teachers have been sending home about you missing assignments and failing tests, your expected low grades shouldn't come as a surprise to anyone.

"That's good." She reaches over and takes a small piece of your doughnut and pops it in her mouth. She chews slowly and takes a sip of her tea. There's something about the way she moves, the way she keeps her eyes on the doughnut, that tells you she's as uncomfortable with this as you are.

When did *that* start? One day you were sitting on her lap playing Candy Land, the next you were a couple of strangers living in the same house, a reality show that's stumbling along until it's canceled. It's not that you don't love her anymore, it's just that everything's changed. But you're not sure how yet, and neither is she. That's why it's so strange.

"How's everything else?"

Good question. "Okay, I guess."

She's trying—you've got to give her credit for that. You know she's fighting the urge to get on you about your grades or finding a job or any one of the other things she's genetically programmed to harass you about. And you'd like to help, but you don't know what to say, either. Tell her how you have no real friends? How you can't work up the balls to ask Ashley out? How you're afraid that you really are going to be as big a failure as everyone seems to think you're going to be? How everything's changing so fast, but nothing's changing at all, that it could be like this for the rest of your life? How sometimes you just want to haul off and punch something?

"Thanksgiving's this Thursday. Don't forget, we're going to Uncle Kevin and Aunt Mary's house."

"Okay."

"They're deep-frying the turkey again this year. You like it like that, don't you?"

"Yeah."

"Remember last year how he almost burned down the garage with that thing?" She laughs and you nod.

"Yeah."

More silence, a second doughnut, then she cracks.

"Kyle, you never picked up a job application from the grocery store. They're not going to come to the door and ask you if you want a job. Now today your father saw a sign at Marello's gas station. You could even walk there. I mean, how hard could it be? But nobody's going to even consider you until you get that résumé finished."

Ten minutes later she wraps up the "clothes that fit" portion of her chat and lets you head up to your room.

You make a mental note not to come home early again.

You flick through all the channels one more time before deciding that Saturday-morning television sucks.

The cartoons are nothing but half-hour commercials for action figures, interrupted every six minutes with actual commercials for the same action figures. It was that way when you were younger and you can't believe you actually used to get up early to watch this crap. If you don't count the sports, the news, the infomercials, the black-and-white movies, the religious programs, or the home-remodeling shows—and you don't—there's nothing on.

If it had been a typical Friday night, you'd still be asleep with another four hours to go before you woke up at the crack of noon. But around seven you started to get a headache and had to get up, the first time you had been out of bed before your parents on a weekend since Christmas five years ago.

You're sitting on the couch, wrapped up in the blanket, clicker in one hand, when your sister sits down next to you.

Paige is five years old, she's in kindergarten, and she's the nicest person you know. She's never been whiny or demanding like all the kids you see at the mall, and as far as you know she's never thrown a temper tantrum or punched something just because she was pissed off.

You got all those genes.

You were ten when she was born, just about the point when your parents must have realized that you were going to screw it all up.

Their Plan B.

The way you see it—the way your parents see it—she can do no wrong. The yin to your yang.

She's wearing her pink pajamas, but no socks, and has a bright blue folder in her hands. Without saying anything, you flick open the blanket and toss a section across her legs, reaching over to make sure her toes are covered. She sets the folder on her lap and looks way up at you and waits.

"What channel?"

She smiles her gap-toothed, cute-as-hell smile. "Twenty-two, please."

You flick. It's *Dora the Explorer*—it's always *Dora the Explorer*.

"Thank you."

You watch her watch, her lips moving along to the theme song, her hands clapping together without making a sound.

Every girl is somebody's sister.

You reach over and slide the folder out from

under her tiny hands. "Whatcha got?" You don't notice how your voice changes when you talk to her.

She looks at you and rolls her eyes. Now you're the master of the obvious. "My *folder.*"

"I know that. What's inside?"

Another eye roll. "My *papers.*"

You pull out a stack of papers, all folded and bent and wrinkled, with "Good Job!" and "Great Work!" written between blue and silver and gold stars, with "Paige Chase" printed in fat pencil at the top. You flip through the stack, trying to remember a time when this was tough stuff. Worksheets on the alphabet, short "The cat is very fat" sentences, pages with apples or trucks or birds to be counted—then a sheet with no stars and a red "Oops! Try Again!"

One of these is different. Circle the one that doesn't belong.

There's pictures of a dog, a table, a boy, and a

horse. With a tight-fisted, squiggly line, Paige had circled the boy. And with a quick swoosh of her red felt-tipped marker, the teacher had circled the table, adding a frown face next to Paige's circle.

"That's wrong," Paige said, pointing to her selection. "I was supposed to pick the table because the dog and the boy and the horse are all alive and the table is not."

"Why'd you pick the boy?"

She scrunches up her shoulders. "All the others have four legs and he has two. But that's wrong."

You want to tell her that she's not wrong, that her answer is just as good as the *correct* answer, maybe better. You want to tell her that what's wrong is the whole stupid assignment, that all it teaches kids is that there's *one* way to think, *one* way to act, so that by the time they reach high school all they have to do is look at somebody and they can tell if he's cool or a nerd or a jock or a hoodie. That way if somebody starts thinking for himself, starts acting all weird, like wearing a sport coat to school, they'll be easy to spot.

One of these people is different. Avoid the one that doesn't belong.

You want to tell her all of this, but you don't. She's smart. Smarter than you, probably. You thought her answer was wrong, too, until she explained it.

But she'll grow up, go to high school, and figure it all out on her own. She won't need you there to explain it all to her.

Which is good, because you won't be.

Two in the afternoon, the postman delivers the mail—a cheap advertising newspaper, a credit-card offer for your mom, your dad's *Golf Digest*, and a small, odd-size envelope with your name on it and no return address. You rip it open and pull out a bright pink Hello Kitty card.

Except it's not a real Hello Kitty card because, while you're no Hello Kitty expert, you don't think she usually has a martini glass in one hand and a cigarette in the other.

WE'RE HAVING A PARTY!

SATURDAY NIGHT

493 FOX MEADOW ROAD

COCKTAILS AT 9

DINNER JACKET OPTIONAL

Z

A week ago you would have tossed it out. But that was a long time ago. A lot can change in a week.

It takes you half an hour to walk to his house. You could have asked your mom for a ride, but then she might start asking questions about parental supervision. Better to let her assume you're hanging out in a dark, cold park with your low-life friends than a warm house with no adults around. You don't know there won't be any adults there, but given the invitation, it's a safe bet.

Zack lives on a cul-de-sac. It's the suburban term for a dead end. His house is a lot like yours, a lot like all the others, with a door and windows and a brick walkway lined with those low solar lights that should have been put away when the leaves started to change. There are three cars in the driveway and none look like the kind a parent would drive. You step up on the porch. Inside you can hear people laughing and the muffled sounds of the stereo.

Up till now Zack has just been this kid you went to school with, a kid you bumped into now and then. He stood up for you, and that now meant you had to do the same for him, but that didn't mean you had to hang out with him. Ringing the bell changes things, crosses another line. He goes from being some kid to a guy you know. Not quite friend level, but there'll be a connection.

When people talk about him, you might get mentioned.

Is that what you need right now, you being associated with the school freak?

You think about your options.

And you ring the bell.

A minute later the door opens.

"Mr. Chase, I'm glad to see you made it." Zack reaches out his arm and shakes your hand, careful not to spill his drink, a tall frosted glass topped with a tiny paper umbrella. He's wearing that black sport coat and a white shirt, a black pair of pants and polished black shoes. You, of course, have on your hoodie uniform.

He leads the way through the living room to the kitchen, where an attractive dark-haired girl is slicing a lime. "Careful," Zack says, sliding up alongside the girl, kissing her on the cheek, "I'd hate to have another guest lose a finger." You and the girl exchange mock surprise looks, then she smiles at you as Zack pulls you by your sleeve into the family room at the back of the house.

There's a dozen people scattered around the room, some on the furniture, some on the floor, some standing by the stereo. Right away you notice that there are more girls than guys, something that never happens when you're hanging out at Ryan's house. Nobody looks familiar—even the way they dress and the way they wear their hair looks different from what you're used to, not radically freaky different, just enough to have you notice. A couple of the guys are wearing loud Hawaiian shirts, one guy even has a tie on. The girls have on everything from skintight tank tops to baggy sweaters, and even though it's close to freezing outside, a few are wearing short shorts. There's jazz oozing out of the speakers. Anything else wouldn't fit, but you wonder if anyone actually likes it.

"Friends, Romans, countrymen, lend me your ears."

And now they're all looking at you as Zack stands there next to you, one hand on your shoulder, the other holding up his drink. Someone turns down the music. "You all recall the torrid events that precipitated my swift departure from Crestwood Academy."

You don't. You've heard rumors—everything from stealing the principal's car to blowing up a science lab to running a strip poker club—but you don't know and frankly don't care. Getting kicked out of Crestwood, a private school way on the other side of town, is probably a lot easier than getting kicked out of a public high school like Midlands. You've never even met anyone who went to Crestwood before, but now, apparently, you're in a room full of them.

"And you've no doubt heard of my many

adventures in the wilds of Midlands High. This is Mr. Chase, hero of so many of those adventures. Mr. Chase, these are some losers I know. I assume they all have names. Go find out for me." He gives your shoulder a slap and walks away.

Before you can feel any more embarrassed, one of the girls on the couch scootches over and pats the cushion next to her. Her long blond hair looks white against her black formfitting sweater. A dainty row of silver rings arches along one eyebrow. You sit.

"Nicole," she says, holding out her hand. Her nails are bright red, matching her lipstick.

"Kyle."

Her fingers are warm.

"Your first time to one of Zack's parties?"

You nod.

"Yeah, he can be a bit out there, but at least he's never boring."

You nod again. It's true.

"So you go to Midlands," Nicole says, as if you

were some thrill seeker, living on the edge. She asks you about the school and the classes and the teachers and students you never heard of but that she's pretty certain go there, and you're telling her, exaggerating only a little, when Zack arrives and hands you both drinks—a pink-colored wine for Nicole and a tall, orange-brown drink with a bendy straw for you. You can smell the whiskey a foot away.

"Don't tell me you two are talking about school." He shakes his head in disgust. "That's one of the house rules, no shop talk. Nicole, tell young Chase here how you were born way up in Dawson Creek, Canada, and you, Mr. Chase, you tell her how fascinating she is. She's quite vain, you know, and if you tell her how beautiful she is you'll have her naked in an hour, posing for a webcam. Isn't that right, Nicole?" He smiles at her as he walks off and she smiles back, a cold smile that makes you uncomfortable.

You ask her about Dawson Creek and she tells you, but it seems forced now, and when she reaches for her buzzing phone, walking off to the kitchen to take a call, you're relieved.

It's close to midnight. The jazz is gone, thank god, replaced by some fast-paced European techno. It's better, but not by much. The conversations are louder, more laughter, more swearing, and there's a sweaty sheen to every face. Half-finished drinks are scattered around the room alongside bowls of picked-over potato chips and pretzel crumbs. It's warm and you've got a good buzz on.

The kid with the tie — Mike? Matt? — is slumped down in a recliner, asleep and drooling, and you saw Nicole leave an hour ago, along with the tall kid someone said was her ex. A bunch of new people have arrived since then, mostly couples but a few more unattached females, and, other than the pairings that disappeared into empty parts of the house, everyone is gathered around the two big couches that fill a corner of the room.

You've been talking with Josh and Andrew and Cindi with an *i* and this kid Josh calls Stitch but who everyone else calls TC, and there's that girl from India, Something Singh, who sounds more like she's from England, and Victoria, whose silver tongue stud clicks against her teeth when she talks, and the girl who's going to Aruba for Thanksgiving, and the one who went last year and almost got busted for smoking pot on the beach, and Becca, who's got the hots for Stitch or TC or whoever the hell he is, and the guy who came in late, the one in the JESUS IS MY HOMIE T-shirt who told you to get out while you still could, just before he fell over drunk on the couch.

And at the center of it all, coat still on, drink still in hand, Zack sits on the arm of the couch. Leaning against him is Brooke, the dark-haired girl from the kitchen.

The Girlfriend.

Cindi with an *i* is telling everybody why they should boycott the zoo and the guy with the lop-sided glasses is explaining to the black chick where to find bootleg movies online. Somebody's telling that penguin-in-a-bar joke again. Your upper lip feels numb and the girl sitting next to you smells like an ashtray. Somebody's cell phone goes off and you and cigarette girl bump heads as you reach for your phones and that gets you both laughing, and you may be buzzing, but you're careful not to laugh too loud or too long. She's there with somebody, but you never know. And it wasn't either of your phones anyway, and you laugh again and right then Brooke goes running from the room and she's crying.

"Not cool, Zack," Andrew says, voice low and flat.

"I can't believe you said that," Victoria says, the metal clicking louder than her words.

You look over at Zack.

That smirk.

He shrugs. "If she doesn't want people to know that she sticks her fingers down her throat after every meal, she shouldn't write it down."

"It's her *journal*, Zack," the Aruba-bound girl says. "It's *private*."

Another shrug. "Not very. It was right beside her bed. And besides, it's not as if she cares what you think about her." He takes a sip of his drink. "That was in there too."

Everyone shifts uncomfortably.

Everyone but Zack.

He sighs a fake sigh and stands up.

"Fine. I shall go . . . *apologize*."

Victoria glares up at him. "It doesn't mean anything if you don't mean it."

Zack smiles. "My dear, I *never* mean it." He gives her a wink and that somehow, *somehow*, makes her smile, too.

Zack steps to the center of the room and claps his hands together. "All right, team, here's the game plan. I'm going to go up to my room where the lovely Miss Brooke is crying facedown on the bed. She *could* be in the bathroom. . . ." He acts like he's about to puke and a few people groan and a few more laugh. "In any case, I can't afford more escort-service bills, so this will take some time. Have yourself a nightcap, hit the lights on the way out, and don't bother sending thank-you cards. *Ciao*."

Twenty minutes later, you're walking home alone.

You wake up Sunday morning and you're ready for it.

The bottle of Gatorade, icy cold last night when you set it alongside your bed, is still cool at eight thirty, the carpet around it wet from condensation.

You crack it open and chug half the bottle in deep, gasping gulps. You wash down a couple of Tylenol—out of the bottle and waiting for you— with a slower, controlled swig. The queasiness isn't as bad as you had feared, but the headache is worse. It's better this way. You could fake your way through a headache, but once you started with the dry heaves your parents would start with the questions.

You stripped off your smoky, vodka-splashed jeans and T-shirt last night, burying them under the pile of dirty clothes to mask the smell. It doesn't, but you don't know that. Your mom can always tell, and that's why, after one party-filled weekend last summer, they had you peeing in a cup.

You duck into the bathroom and jump right into the shower. It's cold, but you stand there, the water hitting you full in the face till you feel your cheeks going numb. Then you ease on the hot water. The room fills with steam and you can feel the cobwebs in your head start to clear.

A little.

Was it worth it?

Is it *ever* worth it?

You're trained to say yes, but you never really thought about it.

And given how your head feels this morning, you're not about to start now.

The mall is packed.

Thanksgiving is still half a week away, but there's Santa in the center of the fluffy-white Christmas village where there's normally a fountain. You think you remember how Santa used to arrive on the day after Thanksgiving, but you don't since they've been doing it this way since before you were born. But your parents remember, and every year they go on about how Christmas these days is just an excuse to get people to buy stuff, not like when *they* were kids. Everything was better then—the toys, the TV specials, the shopping, the kids. *Especially* the kids. It's like Christmas music—you only have to hear it one time a year but even that's too often.

You're wearing your best black sneakers, your least baggy jeans, a dark gray shirt with a collar, and—what else?—your hoodie. Only this is the *new* all-black one and even your mother said you looked nice when she dropped you off, excited that you were *finally* going to fill out job applications. You aren't, but it's cold and raining and you knew that that was the only way she'd give you a ride to the mall.

You cut around the food court, past the lame mechanical Santa's Workshop, past the Gap and the Aberzombie and the Spencer's Gifts and the four or five stores in a row that only sell sneakers, then you slow up and look ahead through the crowd to the Piercing Point kiosk in the middle of the mall.

Ashley's handing a customer a bag. She smiles

and says something—probably "thank you, have a nice day"—and you wait a second to see if anyone else goes to the register before you step back into the flow of traffic.

"Hey," you say as you walk up. Real original.

Ashley looks up from the register and does that double-take thing. "Oh my god, Kyle." She looks happy to see you, bouncing a little as she says it. She usually gives you a hug when she sees you, but she's behind the counter and there are probably rules about her stepping outside of the kiosk to give some guy she's not even dating a hug.

"How's it going?" Brilliant, Kyle, just brilliant.

She shrugs. "Okay. I was supposed to work till five, but Shantay says this other girl called in sick so I gotta be here till closing. Kinda sucks."

"Yeah, that sucks."

"You look nice. What are you all dressed up for?"

Two things:

1. She thinks you look nice

      a. That's the best thing anyone's said to you
         in a long time

      b. Your mom said the same thing when she
         dropped you off

      c. But it was your mom so it doesn't count.

2. She thinks this is dressed up for you

      a. This tells you that she notices what you
         normally wear

      b. It also tells you that she thinks what you
         normally wear makes you look like a slob.

"I'm supposed to be looking for a job," you say, and you tell her how you fooled your mom into driving you to the mall. She's not impressed.

"They're looking for help over at Sears," she says. "And there was a sign over at Abercrombie, but that would be a waste of time."

A waste of time because you'd never work there or a waste of time because they'd never hire you? She doesn't say.

She tells you about piercing this little girl's ears

and how the girl wouldn't stop crying and how she felt awful, pushing her lip out to show you, no idea how hot that makes her look, and then she tells you about this coat she saw and how Cici was late on her first day, and oh my god, how nice it was for you to stop by, and then something else about her job that you don't catch. She's laughing and smiling and she reaches out and touches your arm and you decide to do it, now, right here, ask her if she wants to do something sometime, a meaningless phrase that would tell her everything you were trying to say, an open code that everybody understood, that she would understand and then she'd know, right now, forever.

"Excuse me, can you tell me how much these hoop earrings are?"

And it's over.

The woman pointing, Ashley opening the case, reading the little tags, then a second case, then a mother with some bratty kid and a guy in his twenties trying to return something, the sign right above his ugly head saying NO RETURNS, then two more customers and the guy still trying.

The moment over.

Your moment.

Over.

You stand there like a goddamn idiot for ten minutes before you fade away.

JCPenney. Second-floor men's room.

Five punches and you shatter the plastic cover of the paper-towel dispenser, knocking it off the wall.

Your knuckles are scraped and bleeding, but it's not like the bus.

A lot less blood and nobody screaming.

And it's not like that kid you whaled on last winter, the one who was just standing there, not even looking at you.

More like the hole you put in your bedroom wall, the one you covered with that army poster with the flags.

No way your father's gonna rip *that* one down.

Or like the phone you whipped up against the back of the Kmart when your mother called to tell you to come home. You didn't get hurt on that one, just grounded.

Or like the rock you kicked back in July. Or was it August?

That was stupid.

But you had to do it.

Just do it, right?

You don't feel any better—you never do—but that doesn't matter. It had to be done.

It just . . . happens.

You can taste blood. Must have bit down on your lip.

You run your hand under the cold water, then tear off a wad of what's left of the paper towels. You want to kick something, but you don't, the need dying fast.

Still pissed.

Hell yeah.

But it's not the same.

You're long gone before anyone checks on the noise.

Is it still considered a surprise quiz when everybody seems to know about it but you?

1) In the play Romeo and Juliet, *many characters made decisions that caused problems, or made decisions that they later regretted. Discuss a decision made by one of the characters and explain why that person would come to regret making that decision.*

You think you would have remembered something about a quiz, but you're the only one who had that lost look when Ms. Casey did the clear-everything-off-your-desk drill. You were supposed to have read Act Five over the weekend, but you were busy and you assumed that, like every other time you had read what you were supposed to read for homework, Ms. Casey would just go over it all in class anyway. They trained you well and now you'll pay for it.

2) *In Shakespeare's* As You Like It, *a character notes that "All the world's a stage, And all the men and women merely players." To what extent could this be said to be true in* Romeo and Juliet?

Great. A question based on *another* play you didn't read. On the other side of the room, Zack's pen is racing across the paper. You didn't see him before class and given your schedules you probably won't see him for the rest of the day. That's okay with you. You've been thinking a lot since the party—that hangover clearing out your brain—and what you're thinking is that it's time to get your act together, and hanging around with Zack doesn't seem like the way to do it. The others at the party, they had better clothes and went on expensive vacations and were all heading to big-name universities out of state, but they were just as screwed up as you. A few even more screwed up. Hanging around with Zack didn't make their lives any better and you don't see it doing anything for you. So, yeah, you'll get your act together, get a job, probably at the mall, hopefully someplace near the Piercing Point, use the money you earn to buy some new shirts or something, tell Ashley you need a hand picking out what matches. And really, you can't think of one good reason why you'd want to hang around with Zack.

3) Are Romeo and Juliet simply "star-crossed lovers" or are they responsible for their tragic mistakes?

Even if you didn't know the quiz was coming, you knew this question would be on it. No matter what you're reading, Ms. Casey turns it into a lecture on personal responsibility.

A poem? *Discuss how the author inspires readers to take control of their lives.*

A Greek myth? *Show how Odysseus created his own fate.*

A short story? *Explain how the narrator's refusal to assert her free will led to her downfall.*

It's Ms. Casey's favorite topic and you know exactly how to answer it, even if you don't know what you're talking about.

Bonus Question (+5 points): Name five of the

actors besides Leonardo DiCaprio who were

in the movie version we watched last week.

Extra points for knowing some piece of *People*
magazine trivia.

That's your fate.

No wonder you hate this class.

"Hey."

It's Max and he's standing near your locker. You
nod. "Hey."

"What up?"

You spin the combination lock and jerk open the
door.

"Where were you this weekend?"

"I was busy."

"Yeah?"

There's something sharp in his voice that makes

you look over. He's got his arms crossed and he's leaning back against the row of lockers. Max the Tough Guy.

"Ryan says you went to a party at the queer kid's house."

A week ago you'd have been quick with a denial, now it's not worth the effort. You turn back to your locker. "What did *you* do?"

"Derrick found a box of wine in the back of a pickup truck at the 7-Eleven. You should have been there."

"Gee, sounds like fun." Kyle the King of Sarcasm.

Max starts in with the F-bombs, but then he stops midword and the first thing you think is that there's a teacher walking up behind you, so you keep fumbling around in your locker. You're not getting blamed for that one.

"You're Kyle, right?"

There's a hint of spice in the air, expensive and subtle. You turn around slowly.

She's as tall as you, so you're looking right into her eyes. Sky blue eyes, the makeup perfect, the face golden bronze, also perfect, the straight blond hair bouncing below her smooth shoulders, down to her chest. Perfect, perfect, large and perfect. A senior, but not a senior like Jake the Jock. The rare kind of senior, the kind who seems to float through the building, above it all, above the cliques and the gossip, the Senior Class crap and the little school romances all so quaint and foreign to them. The kind who already have jobs in offices or boyfriends in their twenties, new cars and exotic tastes, the kind who never work hard in school but whose names are called over and over at honors ceremonies, the kind who are never there to pick up their Xeroxed awards. Always girls—no, always *women*—and always stunning. Not teenage adorable, not high-school pretty. Stunning. Girls like this don't talk to guys like you, don't know that you live on the same planet as they do.

"Victoria said she met you the other night at Zack's," she says while you stand there with your jaw on the floor.

"She said you were a cutie." She smiles the kind of smile that tells you to forget it, you're way out of your league. But still, she's talking to you.

"So, you have a good time?"

You nod. "Um, yeah. Yeah it was fun." Kyle the Idiot.

She gives a perfect little laugh. "They always are. Did he make you one of his margaritas? You gotta watch those, they sneak up on you."

You give a stupid little laugh, nodding like a bobblehead.

"And I hear he got Brooke crying." She rolls her eyes. "Not that that's hard."

"Yeah, that was kinda, I don't know, mean."

"That's our Zack. He finds your weak spot, then keeps pushing till you crack. Still"—she shrugs—"he makes a good margarita."

She laughs and you laugh because you don't know what else to do. You *should* ask her what else she knows about Zack, things like what he did to get kicked out of that school and how he gets away with throwing parties at his house and what he's done to other people when he finds their weak spots. But you won't. Girls like this don't talk to guys like you, and when one actually does, you don't start asking questions about some other guy.

"Right, I gotta go," she says, checking the time on the cell phone she's not supposed to have in school. "Let me know the next time Zack's having a party. I'll give you a lift."

She walks off and naturally you watch her go. That's perfect too.

You turn back to your open locker and Max is staring at you, his eyes wide at first, then they narrow and you can guess what he's thinking.

One word from you and it'd be okay, everything back to normal, back to the way it was.

But you just look at him and smile.

No, not smile.

You smirk.

It makes no sense kicking a kid out of class for not doing his homework.

Maybe he was busy actually doing in-class work when the assignment was supposedly given, or maybe the teacher wasn't as clear as she claims she was. There's the chance that he heard the assignment and chose not to do it and take the zero, but a better chance that *if* he heard it he just forgot about it, that he doesn't want the zero and certainly doesn't need it. But he'll get one anyway. So now the kid's behind, but if he pays attention in class he might be able to piece it together and catch up. After all, it's only one fill-in-the-blank worksheet. It would make sense to keep him in there. The teacher could give him detention, or better yet, give him a break for once, let it slide, but that never happens and the kid gets kicked out of class, sent to see the vice principal. And when he comes to class the next day, guess what? He won't have *that* day's homework.

In any case, it makes no sense. And this is what you're thinking as you hand the preprinted form to the vice principal's secretary and she tells you to take a seat in the long row of empty chairs that line one wall of the office.

Like you haven't done it a thousand times before.

The VP's door is shut, but you don't think there's anyone in there. She may not even be in the building and you may end up sitting here for the whole morning, forced to listen to the secretary's radio, set to a station the DJ calls "adult contemporary." Maybe that's the punishment. You've heard that the secretary can write a pass, get you out of seeing the

VP and send you off to your next class, but out of all your trips to this office—and there've been a lot of them—it hasn't happened yet. And you don't think it's going to start today. You put your head back and slouch down in the seat and settle in for a nap, but your eyes aren't closed ten seconds before three sharp raps on the outer office door let you know that you have company.

"Zachary McDade, reporting as ordered."

It figures.

You glance over and he's standing with his back to you, facing the secretary's desk, his right arm sweeping up in a theatrical military salute. The secretary laughs—why, you don't know. "Zachary, *what* are we going to do with you?" She's said the same thing to you before, but she wasn't laughing when she said it.

"Oh, Mrs. Clevenger. You *know* I'm your favorite." You can hear the wink in his voice and you can't believe she'd buy it, but she does. She says something witty to him and he says something back, and then she says something else and they both laugh, and you're wondering where he learned to talk to adults. A simple conversation, nobody yelling, just talking. If an adult talked to you like that, you wouldn't know what to say. But that's all right, adults don't talk to you. They talk at you.

He says one last line that you don't catch but that the secretary thinks is hilarious, then turns to take a seat and spots you. He looks surprised and, if you didn't know better, happy to see you.

"Chase, my good man. Fancy meeting you here." He makes his way down the row of empty chairs, and as he leaves an open chair between you when he sits, you realize that there are some unwritten rules that even he won't break. "So," he says, "what mortal sin did you commit?"

"I didn't do my homework."

"Horrors!" he says, louder than he should have, one hand on his chest, the other covering his eyes, and . . . . you laugh. You didn't mean to, it's not that funny, it just happened. You make a mental note not to let it happen again.

"My sins are not as horrific," he says, "but I'll still have to talk to a counselor. She'll ask me the same questions they always do—why must I be so disruptive, why must I be the center of attention, why must I be so controlling. And I'll tell her what I always tell them—broken home, absent father, drunken mother, inferiority issues, loneliness, fear of the dark. . . ."

You have to ask. "How much is true?"

"Do you really care?"

You say no—and you don't—but admit it, you *are* curious.

He sighs a loud, dramatic sigh and looks over to see if the secretary notices. She doesn't, too busy shuffling papers as she talks on the phone, a one-sided conversation about her husband's cholesterol that doesn't sound like school business.

"If I told them the truth, the real reason I am the wonderful way that I am, they wouldn't believe me."

You know he wants you to ask, so you don't. He tells you anyway.

"I'm bored out of my mind, Chase. Do you understand? Out of my mind. And why? Because it's all so mindlessly, ridiculously, insultingly, *painfully* easy. All of it. Easy."

For him. Acing tests, getting girls, punking jocks, conning adults. No sweat. Nothing is easy to you, but you'd never tell him that. And he's not really talking to you, anyway. He's talking at you.

"It's a game, Chase. A big boring game. If you play by the rules like they tell you, you win. But who wants to play a game that *everybody* wins? It's more of a challenge to make them play *my* game. Teachers, parents, counselors, girls who should know better, and guys who never do. Everybody. They play my game. And that's why we win."

We?

"That's my story, Chase. Bored Teen Struggles to Stay Sane. What I don't understand is what you're doing here."

"I told you. I didn't do the homework."

"Not here in this *room*, Chase, here in this *school*. Mediocre Midlands High. It makes no sense."

Yes it does. It's the only thing that makes sense. But now he's got you wondering what he means. Not that you'd ask. Instead, you shrug. Let him guess what you mean.

"I fear it's only a matter of time until you are as bored with it all as I am," he says, watching the secretary out of the corner of his eye as she gathers up some papers and heads out the door, leaving you two alone in the room. "By then I will have worn out my Midlands welcome and will have been shipped off to another school. Yes, young Chase, one day all this will be yours. Now, if you'll be so kind as to watch the hallway . . . ."

He moves quickly to the secretary's desk, waving you up with him as he goes. You know what he's doing and you follow, taking position by the door.

"Whistle if you see anything," he says, riffling through a stack of folders.

You look down the hall. It's empty, but you can hear the sound of clicking heels echoing around the corner. "Make it quick," you say without turning.

"Here we go. The *official* detention list." He takes a black pen from the desk and scribbles something on the page. "And now we are *officially* pardoned."

You step back from the door and look at the paper, a passable copy of the principal's signature after your name, releasing you from a week's worth of detention. Out in the hall, the clicking heels move closer. You head for your seat, but Zack catches your arm.

"Oh look—one day of detention for my *dear* friend Jessica Savage. You don't know her. A senior. Invited to my party, did not show." He taps the list in time with the approaching steps.

"You can't sign us all out," you tell him as you lean away. You don't want to be found anywhere near the secretary's desk.

"I have no intention of pardoning Miss Savage. In fact, I think she needs to be taught a lesson." He makes a quick mark, changing the one to a four.

Ten seconds later the secretary returns and you're back in your seats. When the bell rings, Zack asks politely, and she writes you both passes to your next class.

Your uncle Kevin bows his head. "Lord, You have given us so much to be thankful for. . . ."

Five things you are thankful for:

1. Online gaming
2. Ways around the lame porn filter your father put on your computer

3. Ultimate Fighting marathons on Spike TV

4. Ashley

5.

"You're probably wondering how long we have before the alarm goes off."

You're standing next to Zack in front of a beeping keypad mounted on the wall inside the maintenance entrance of Midlands High School, and that's exactly what you're wondering.

The beeping started when you came out of the dark classroom, the motion detectors picking you up with your first step into the empty corridor where the foreign-language classes are all clustered together. During the three days of school that led up to Thanksgiving break, the French teacher focused on conjugating verbs while Zack concentrated on disabling the window's locks.

"You'd think the tricky part would be to make it look as if it's locked when it's not," he had pointed out after you had both slipped through the window and pulled it shut behind you, careful not to drop the tire iron. "But the fact is, people don't expect things to change. If it was locked last week, it'll be locked today. It's an assumption that makes my life so much easier."

You stayed low, letting your heartbeat slow back down, quieting your breathing, certain that someone would come busting into the room. But no one did and after five minutes you were ready to move on.

Now, just seconds later, Zack has you standing in front of the keypad. He's got a hold of your elbow, keeping you centered, but you're not trying to get away. Not yet anyway.

"You see, Mr. Chase, this alarm, like most entry alarms you'll encounter, has a delay before it triggers the main alarm. That's the beeping you hear. It gives you time to punch in the code number to deactivate the alarm. And notice that the small red LED at the top is now on."

"Turn it off."

"Well, that requires the code. Without the code the main alarm will sound, the emergency lights will go on, and the police will be here in seconds." He gives a nod in the direction of the keypad. "It's *very* efficient."

"Turn it off." You raise your voice to be heard over the beeps.

"Notice anything unusual about the keypad?"

"Don't be an ass. Turn it off." The beeps are getting louder and faster, or does it just seem that way?

Zack ignores you. "There are twelve keys, arranged like a phone. Most codes for alarms are four digits. But which four?"

You feel your teeth grinding together, the beeps definitely louder. "Turn it off. Now."

"In the light of day I noticed that five of the keys are smudged—the four, the six, the eight, and the zero, along with the star key. Obviously, these are the keys most often pushed. Star will be the last key, but what is the *order* of the rest? Had me puzzled all through physics class."

The red LED starts flashing. You pull your elbow free and glare at him in the dim light.

"Simple logic tells us that the code would have to be something that everyone authorized to enter the building could easily remember. If you haven't noticed, teachers are not an overly bright lot."

You can feel your fist tighten and you know what's coming.

"But then I realized where I had seen the numbers—the last four digits of the school's phone number. Eight, six, zero, four." He punches the keys as he says the numbers. "And then star and, *voilà!*"

The beeping stops, the red LED goes off.

Your teeth are still clenched.

"Well, Mr. Chase, that was close."

Yes, it was.

"Come," he says, swinging the tire iron up on his shoulder. "On with the mission."

There's something different about the school at midnight. The fluorescent lights are on during the day, but they only add to the natural light that floods through the windows. At night they give the hallways an eerie glow. The windows on the classroom doors are black, hiding everything inside. The only sound is the rush of air from the vents overhead. It's a different building at night.

You notice it because, for the first time, you feel welcome here.

You're surprised at how little noise you make walking down the hall. Even Zack is quiet, both of you listening for a door to open or a distant footfall. You take the stairs to the second floor, Zack leaning forward to scope out the hallway before you continue. You come around the corner and freeze, a square-jawed Marine in dress blues saluting you from behind a glass door.

"It scares me, too," Zack says, pointing the tire iron at the life-size cardboard cutout in the career center. "I think it's the two different blues. Not natural."

It's stupid, but you laugh and the tension is broken. You start walking and there's a lightness to your step. You're still alert—maybe more so—but now you're not nervous. Now you're having fun.

"Here we are, Mr. Chase. Locker one seventy-four."

It looks like any other locker in the row—lime green, five feet tall, ten inches wide, a built-in combination lock next to the chrome latch. No decals on the front, no graffiti. Nothing that says THIS LOCKER BELONGS TO JAKE THE JOCK.

"Are you—"

"Yes, I'm positive it's his," Zack says. "I observed the lummox at this locker several times this past week."

"And you're sure it's not his girlfriend's?"

"Locker three fourteen. And remember, there's a school rule against sharing lockers."

You reach out for the tire iron. "Probably should come at it low."

"Yes. Don't want to pop the lock. That would give it all away."

You slip the flat end in the slim gap between the locker door and the frame.

"Gently. Don't bend the metal."

With careful pressure, you bow out the door, creating a thin opening, a sliver of light shining in on a sweater and a stack of books.

"Here." You move your hands out of the way so Zack can grip the tire iron. Then you unzip your fly.

Zack leans back and looks away but keeps the locker pried open. "Aren't you glad I had you chug that Gatorade?"

You've got good aim. You can hear the warm stream soaking the sweater and splashing down the books, a metallic ring as it finds the back wall of the locker.

Zack edges farther away. "Watch it. Stay focused on the task in hand."

It takes a satisfyingly long time, but you finish and zip up. Zack eases the door closed, stepping around the growing yellow puddle at the foot of the locker.

"See?" he says. "I told you it would be worth it."

And he's right.

Mission accomplished, you backtrack your way through the building. If you had tried something like this with Max or Derrick, somehow it would have gone wrong, with Max stuck in a window or Derrick making phone calls the whole time. And if it had been Ryan he wouldn't have been happy until he'd smashed TVs and ripped up books.

This way was best. Adventurous. Almost classy.

It feels right.

So maybe life doesn't suck so bad after all.

Until Zack stops in front of Ashley's locker.

"This is your girlfriend's locker, isn't it? Miss Bianchi?"

You wish, but you don't tell him that. You don't need to, since he obviously knows.

"She's not my girlfriend," you say, and as you say it your stomach folds in on itself and your chest turns to lead and there's a taste in your mouth like you're about to puke and you don't know why.

Zack's eyebrows arch up too far. *"Really?* Gosh, I didn't know."

He knew.

"Wow. She's so darn cute. And you're such a nice guy. . . ."

But maybe not nice enough.

"It's a shame, you'd be perfect together," he says, and you're not looking at him, but you can see him shake his head, overacting on purpose just to make it worse. "Are you *sure* you're not a couple?"

"Yeah, I'm sure."

He *tsk, tsk, tsks*, and adds an exaggerated sigh. "Really and truly, cross your heart and hope to die?"

You choose an appropriate F-word response, delivering it with a casual nonchalance that you hope will end the discussion, hard to do through gritted teeth.

"Fine, fine," he says, putting his hands up in mock defense as you start walking away. "Sooo . . . if she's *not* your girlfriend you wouldn't mind if I called her, right?"

You glance over at him and you're thinking:

Wrong.

She wouldn't talk to you.

She wouldn't have anything to do with someone like you.

You don't even know what she's like.

You wouldn't treat her right.

You're not her type.

Don't.

You start back down the hallway toward the stairs and foreign-language classrooms and over your shoulder you say:

"Do whatever you want."

You hear a chuckle. "I always do."

HOW YOU GOT THAT SCAR ON THE BACK OF YOUR HAND PART 3: WHAT YOU TOLD ASHLEY IN HOMEROOM ON MONDAY

Yeah, you *do* remember.

Last year, in March.

Yeah, on the bus.

I told you before.

You sure?

Oh.

I don't like to talk about it.

I just don't.

I don't know.

Okay, but don't tell anybody I told you.

Just because, okay?

Do you want to hear or not?

Promise?

All right, so some asshole was making fun of this retarded kid—

I don't know, just some asshole.

I think he transferred or something.

He was saying crap, you know, about the retard.

Sorry.

Anyway, I'm sitting across from him and I go, shut the hell up—

Yeah, more than that, of course.

Well, because you don't like when people swear.

Yeah, real frickin' sweet.

So anyway, he keeps it up and I'm like, shut the hell up, and he's like, what are you gonna do, so I stand up and go to punch him in the head—

I don't know, tenth grade maybe.

About my size, maybe bigger.

No, he was bigger than that.

I didn't care, he was making fun of the retard.

Sorry.

So I stand up and just as I'm swinging, the bus swerves and I go flying and put my hand through the window.

Yeah, blood everywhere.

He freaked.

Naw, didn't hurt.

Twelve stitches.

I told them I slipped.

He was too scared to say anything.

The retarded kid?

I guess he still goes here, I don't know.

Back in March.

A couple days after your birthday.

Yeah, I heard it was a good time.

No, I wasn't there.

I'm sure.

I was probably busy anyway.

Yeah, that happens with emails sometimes.

No, it's cool.

Why would I have been pissed?

It was just a party.

Yeah, this year for sure.

You turn the corner to walk down the hall—*the hall*—toward the *scene of the crime*. There's a small crowd standing around locker 174.

Well, not *that* close around.

And there's Jake, jacking some freshman up against the wall with one hand. His signature move. It's a small crowd, their freakish size making it look bigger, and you keep walking right toward it.

"Why you laughing, huh? What's so funny, huh?" It's Jake, making a new friend.

"I-I-I didn't . . . I don't . . . I-I . . ." says the freshman.

"You think it's *funny*?"

Jake's friends definitely think it is. They're laughing so hard that no teacher would ever think that in the middle of that beefy crowd some poor freshman is about to have his nose broken. Even the students walking by smile, the laughter infectious. You'd smile, too, if you weren't fighting to keep a straight face.

"I said, you think it's funny?"

Then somebody says, "Leave him alone, he didn't do anything."

Surprise.

It's you.

Jake turns, releasing his death grip on the anonymous freshman, who slips out from under Jake's thigh-size arm. Jake looks at you and blinks, either trying to place the face or imagine what kind of idiot would tell him what to do.

Probably both.

His friends are still bent over laughing as he takes a half step toward you.

"You do this?" he says, pointing back at the open locker door. The sweater is on the floor, but the books are still stacked inside, the curled edges looking like a dried-up waterfall. And there's the smell.

"Do what?" You can still sound innocent when you have to.

His eyes widen and he jabs his finger a second time. "Did you piss in my locker?"

You're sure he didn't mean to do it, but Jake reduces his friends to tears, two of them actually on the floor, holding their sides, all of them crying now, gasping between howls of laughter.

And here's where you have to think.

Too much smart-ass in your voice and you are dead, right here, in front of everybody. And too little backbone in your answer and you might as well die, right here in front of everybody.

You choose the sarcastic but still friendly

voice. It's a safe choice.

"Yeah," you say, "it was me. You got me. Yup, I broke into the school, bypassed the alarm, opened your locker, and pissed in it."

You look right at him as you say it and now everybody is laughing at the ridiculousness of it all. Kyle Chase? Break into school? Bypass an alarm just to pee in a locker? Oh my *god*, that's funny!

And you smile, too. Not a smirk, you're not that stupid. Just a friendly, almost silly smile, the kind a grandmother would find sweet.

You've gone and confused him. He reels from side to side, ready to explode but lost, no idea where to strike out. You'd know what to do in this situation, how to just punch out at the wall or the locker or something without thinking, but you don't believe he's open to suggestions right now, so you just turn and walk away, Jake's jock friends even step out of the way to let you pass, laughing so hard they probably can't see straight.

Ms. Casey is standing in front of the class explaining how she worked all weekend to get the tests graded so she could hand them back Monday morning, and you're wondering if you're supposed to be impressed that she did her job.

"Overall, most of you did the level of work you've been doing all year. No big surprises there. However," she says, beaming as she draws the word out, "one student in this class earned a perfect score—and that's *before* the bonus." She pauses, as if expecting you all to burst into cheers. When you don't she continues, a bit disappointed by the general lack of excitement over the miraculous event.

"When a student earns a perfect score on a test it goes to show that the information was clearly covered and that the test was more than fair."

And now you understand. The perfect score isn't due to exceptional student achievement, it's all because of her brilliant teaching methods.

"I know that all of you are capable of better work.

Well, all but *one* of you, I suppose." She chuckles at her little joke. "That's why I decided to grade this test—and everything from this point on—just a bit harder. That means you'll have to work a little harder, but as that perfect test score shows, you can do it."

You want to raise your hand and ask Ms. Casey if she thinks it's fair to change the rules in the middle of the game or if she thinks it's fair to judge the whole class by what one geek did on one test, but you don't because you know she'll say it *is* fair and that if you simply took more responsibility for your learning you could whatever, and on and on till she got you pissed enough where you'd say something smart-assed and it's not worth it, any of it, so you say nothing, busy adding UCK to the big red F on your paper.

Forty-six minutes later you join the crowd working its way through the door and out of Ms. Casey's class when Zack falls in next to you, stuffing his notebook in his backpack as he walks.

"Young Mr. Chase. How goes your day?"

You shrug.

"How'd you do on that little quiz?"

You shrug again. "About what I expected."

"Me too," he says, still fumbling with his note-book. "The lovely Ms. Casey tried to rip me off of one of my bonus points because I put down Lupita Ochoa, but she must have gone back and checked. Anyway, I like the Zeffirelli version better. There's a topless scene with Juliet. Right. Off to math. Later."

He turns left out the door, you head right, but not before you see the test paper in his backpack, the word *perfect* printed in red ink along the top of the page.

"Don't slouch, you'll get your shirt more wrinkled than it is. And when you shake someone's hand, don't have a limp grip. Nothing turns people off faster than a weak handshake. I knew we should have practiced shaking hands before we left the house."

It's three o'clock on Monday afternoon. You're wearing your best sneakers and a pair of pants you never would have bought. You're also wearing a polo shirt, something else you never would have bought, but at least it's black. What you're not wearing is a hoodie. It's warm out and it's supposed to stay that way for the next couple of days. Besides, you're ready for a change.

In your lap is a crisp new manila folder containing two copies of your unimpressive résumé. Your mother is giving you last-minute instructions as she drives you to the mall.

Obviously, this was not your idea.

"And don't say *yeah*, say *yes*. And don't roll your eyes like that."

She was waiting for you when you got home from school, noting—before the front door was even shut—that (a) you have not found a job yet, (b) they are done talking to you about it, (c) no one is going to come to the house to offer you a job, and (d) you're going to apply at Sears today. Apparently your father is sick and tired of waiting for you to get off your lazy ass and get a job. Not the words your mom used when she told you, but you know that's what he said.

"Don't ask about the pay. It'll be minimum wage if anything. I just don't know why you waited this long."

Your sister, Paige, is in the backseat, playing with the loose end of her seat belt. She's singing something to herself and you're trying to figure out what it is, but your mother is distracting.

"And don't say that you don't have any work experience. Tell them how you shovel driveways in the winter. And you used to cut Mr. Frances's lawn until you . . . well, it's probably best if you just don't mention that."

The last time you shoveled driveways you were in sixth grade. And it's not your fault that Mr. Frances never told you about the flower garden. And that was five years ago. You want to tell her these things— and you want to tell her how you don't want to work at Sears, that you don't want to wear khaki pants and polo shirts, but the minivan is pulling up to the mall and it wouldn't have made any difference anyway.

She rolls down the window as she pulls away, telling you to smile.

You can't think of a single reason why.

You cut around the food court, past the lame mechanical Santa's Workshop, past the Gap and the Aberzombie and the Spencer's Gifts and the four or five stores in a row that only sell sneakers, then you slow up and look ahead through the crowd to the Piercing Point kiosk in the middle of the mall.

Déjà vu.

It's Monday, but the mall's still crowded, and they're standing three deep at the Piercing Point. Ashley is helping a guy your father's age buy a pair of earrings. When she looks down into the case in front of her, you notice that he's trying to look down her top. Not that she has a lot to look at, but still. He's probably got a daughter her age. He ends up buying a few pairs and while she rings him up, you stroll over and stand near the register.

"Oh my god, it's sooo busy," Ashley says after the man leaves. "I can't talk now. You look nice. Call me, okay? Before eleven. Gotta go." She does one of those air kisses, then turns to help some woman.

And now you are smiling.

"Kyle, I have to tell you, I'm impressed."

You're sitting in an office in the customer-service area at Sears, near the bathrooms and the photo studio and the counters where people are making credit-card payments, and the guy interviewing you is sitting behind a desk that can't be his, not with the stuffed animals on top of the computer terminal and the collection of cat postcards tacked up on the bulletin board. All you did was ask for a job application but instead of just handing you the form and letting you walk away like you had planned, this guy appeared and said that he'd like to interview you now if it was convenient. You couldn't think of a reason why it wasn't—at least not fast enough—so here you are.

"Not many kids your age think to bring a résumé when they pick up an application," he says, holding it up as if he were presenting it to the court. "You know what that tells me? It tells me that you think ahead, that you plan for the unexpected. And it tells me that you're conscientious. You notice details. *And*, most important, it tells me you really want this job. Now tell me, am I right?"

He's not, but he's on a roll. You just smile and nod, and that makes him smile and nod.

"When I was your age—"

Here it comes.

Is it possible that it's genetics? Something gets triggered when you hit a certain age, like a form of puberty, but for adults? At thirteen, it's hairy underarms and an obsession with sex. At forty, it's hair in your ears and an uncontrollable urge to tell people how things were better when they were a kid. Only with puberty you pass through it in a couple of years. This adult thing, when it hits, lasts the rest of your life.

He covers the usual points: clothing, music, hairstyles, chores, jobs, school, church, Scouts, cars, and respect.

"So tell me, Kyle," he asks, "how are you doing in school?"

So you tell him. Why not? He'd probably call anyway.

He stares at you. And keeps staring at you. You're about to stand up and walk out when he says, "Good for you." Not a condescending "good for you," the kind your father says when you mention that you've jumped three levels on an online game. He really means it, and now you're staring at him.

"See, Kyle, most kids your age would lie. Okay, maybe not lie. They'd stretch the truth a bit or maybe blame the teachers, all that crap. You? You told the truth. Kids with good grades we've got. *Honest* kids? That's something else."

Now comes the standard hard-work/rags-to-riches/lots-of-opportunities-for-those-who-try speech, and you zone out a bit until you can sense it's wrapping up. You sit a little straighter, mostly because your back is starting to hurt.

"I like what I see here, Kyle," he says, tapping your worthless résumé. "I'm sure we'll have a few more applicants, but I'll tell you right now, I doubt I'll see anyone as good as you."

You're thinking, he has to be kidding, but apparently he's not, and the next thing he's walking you back to the service desk, telling you about the break room and how you'll have an ID card.

"I can tell a lot by a handshake," he says, working your arm like it's a pump handle. "I can tell you'll do fine here."

Before he goes back to the office, he asks if you can stop back tomorrow, say around four. You say yes and the interview is over.

You said exactly twelve words.

You don't want to walk past the Piercing Point again—well, you do, but you know you can't—

so you go the long way around the mall, past the Banana Republic and the pretzel place, and past what's supposed to be Santa's stable, complete with nine mechanical reindeer, one with a flashing red nose. Much more interesting, however, are the life-size photographs of sleepy-eyed models in red negligees in the store's windows. So interesting in fact that you walk right into Nicole as she comes out of Victoria's Secret.

It takes you both a second, but then you remember that night at Zack's party. You remember her talking about Canada and growing up in Dawson Creek. She smiles at you, a beautiful smile, and then you can't help but think about what Zack said about the webcam.

She holds up two armloads of bags. "Getting my Christmas shoplifting done early."

You laugh, wondering if it's true.

"I wish you were here ten minutes ago. I was

trying on a bathing suit and could have used a second opinion."

You make some lame comment about how you're sure it looked great and then she says no and you say yeah and now you can't stop thinking about the webcam.

"So," she says, stretching the word out as she shifts her grip on the bags, "did he figure it out yet?"

You give her that blank look.

"Zack. Did he figure it out yet?"

"Figure what out?"

She sighs, but she's still smiling. Obviously the boy is a bit slow. "Your weakness. How to get to you."

You remember what that girl told you at school, the perfect senior who liked margaritas.

He finds your weak spot, then keeps pushing till you crack.

He pushed Brooke until she cried. And what he

said to Nicole pushed her out of the house and into your fantasies.

But . . .

It's different for guys.

Everybody knows that.

A guy pushes you, you punch back.

End of story.

"He gets to everybody. He'll get to you. Trust me, he'll figure you out."

You shrug. "There's nothing to figure out."

"Funny." Her smile shifts—not quite a smirk but not as warm as it had been. "That's what I said too."

You're lying on your bed, lights off, hands behind your head, staring up at the ceiling. You're still wearing the clothes you wore to the job interview—you were supposed to hang them up right away, but it's not like you're going on another one in the morning or something.

It's early. Eight, maybe eight thirty. Too early to call Ashley. You could go downstairs and watch TV, but your father's watching that shouting guy again. Now and then a "shut up" cuts through the mumbling white noise, either your father or the TV guy, you can't tell. You could go watch the other TV, but there's never anything good on, and walking that far doesn't seem worth the effort.

What you'd like to do is play an online game, maybe World of Warcraft or Fallen Earth, but your computer is missing, one of your father's brilliant motivation techniques. It seems you have to *earn* the right to have a computer in your room. And they think you didn't do any homework before?

So you lie there.

You do this a lot, this lying on your bed, lights off, hands behind your head, staring up at the ceiling. It's what you do when you think about things. Not things like school or getting a job or your future.

You do your best not to think about them at all.

What you think about are sold-out concerts and you up on the stage, or leading a ninja death squad into a shogun castle, or gun battles with alien predators, or racing stolen Ferraris through the streets of LA, a hardcore soundtrack shredding your ears.

Oh, by the way, your iPod? That's gone too.

But mostly you think about Ashley.

Is that why you keep your hands behind your head?

So you're lying on your bed, lights off, etc., and instead of listening to music you're listening to your mom talking to Paige as she gets your sister ready for bed.

"I don't wanna wear the blue dress to school tomorrow."

"I thought it was your favorite?"

"Uh-uh. The pink one is my favorite."

"You just wore the pink one today. You have to

wear something different tomorrow."

"Kyle wears the same shirt every day."

Technically, she's wrong. They may look like the same black T-shirt, but they're different.

"That's Kyle," your mom says.

"I wanna be like Kyle when I grow up."

There's a pause—and you're thinking, does she mean the clothes or something else, something she sees in you that no one else sees, that you don't see, something she likes, something no one else has, something that means the world to her?

Then your mom says, "No, Paige, you do not want to be like Kyle. One in a family is enough."

Your breathing changes first. Short, choppy breaths pulled in and out through flaring nostrils.

Next your jaw muscles lock up, then your teeth grind.

Your fists are held so tight your knuckles crack one by one.

She could have said anything.

Any damn thing.

But she said that.

To Paige.

And you're . . . what?

Pissed?

Hurt?

Embarrassed?

Betrayed?

Yeah.

All of those.

Because it's unfair?

Or . . .

Because it's true?

"Oh my god, Kyle, you called. I was worried you'd forget."

You're standing in the darkened kitchen, leaning against the door to the garage, the telephone cord stretched across the room, trying to sound casual without being overheard. Normally you'd be up in your room with the door shut, talking on your cell phone, but that's another thing you have to earn back. And you're thinking, there's no way I'd forget to call you, but what you say is, "I just remembered."

"I'm glad. Did you get the message I left on your phone?"

And yet another reason to be pissed at your father. You tell her no, hinting at your father's latest hobby.

She laughs. "Sounds like my mom and her stupid phone rules."

And you laugh. You know all about stupid rules.

"Sorry I couldn't talk when you came by. We were so busy. What were you all dressed up for?"

You tell her about the job interview at Sears, but after twenty seconds you hear her mom saying something in the background, then Ashley saying something about there still being like five whole minutes, and when she comes back with an eye-rolling "sorry," you jump to the end. "Anyway, I gotta see him tomorrow. I think I got the job."

"Really?" she says, and she sounds either surprised or disappointed. There's a two-beat pause, followed by a distracted "huh," then another pause, and the silence is roaring in your head, so you ask her how her job was because you know that will get her talking.

"Okay," she says. Then that damn pause again, this time with a sigh.

Your stomach is starting to roll up, squeezing the air out of your lungs, your gut way ahead of your mind.

"Kyle?"

Pause.

"Yeah?"

Pause.

"I gotta ask you something."

Pause.

"Yeah?"

Pause.

"You and me, we're tight, right?"

Tight.

As in close?

As in intimate?

Or as in friends?

"Okay, Mom, I *know!*" she shouts as she tilts the phone away, not far enough really. "*Jeez.* Anyway"—another sigh, the kind that says she's waiting for her mom to leave—"I gotta talk to you about something."

You swallow. "Yeah?"

"I've been thinking . . . lately I've been, like . . . this is *so* embarrassing . . . okay . . . so, like . . . you and me . . . ugh, this was *so* much easier just leaving you a message . . . I wanna tell you . . . ."

I love you.

That's gotta be it.

That's what she's going to say, you can feel it.

Okay, maybe not love, but something like love, something close enough.

And you're hanging there, waiting for it, knowing it's coming, and you hear a loud voice say, "Right now, young lady. You know the rule."

Then a sigh.

"Sorry, Kyle. I gotta go."

Two minutes later, a recorded voice tells you that it appears that there is a phone off the hook, asking you to check your extensions. You listen to the message three times before you hang up.

You blame your father for your being late for school.

For the past six months you've been using your cell phone as an alarm clock. You had to, since your regular alarm clock somehow threw itself against the wall one afternoon. On school days you're always the first one out of bed, and since you're "so damn noisy in the morning, Kyle," no one else bothers to set an alarm.

But no cell phone, no alarm.

And this is why, fifty minutes after the bus passed by your house, you're sitting in the front seat of your father's Bronco as he drives you to school. He's running late too. He hasn't said a word to you all morning. You know he blames you and you expected to hear all about it the whole way to school, but he's got the radio cranked up, listening to the shouting shut-up guy. His role model.

It's eight minutes from your house to the school and you both ride in silence, but when your father pulls the Bronco up to the front of the school and you start to climb out, he finally says something to you.

"Don't slam the damn door."

You walk into school and start down the hall to sign in, and absolutely nothing seems different or out of the ordinary. Tomorrow, however, everyone will claim that today felt funny right from the start. And that you looked somehow different. But as you glance at your reflection as you walk past the school's trophy case, all you see is the same old you.

So it's Tuesday morning—a B day on the screwed-up rotation schedule. That means PE class. You're late, but since you had to wait on your father to drive you, you have your gym stuff ready for a change, and you hit the weight room only ten minutes late.

Your gym teacher is Mr. Matlock, and he's cool about things like this. He'd say good morning and you'd hand him the note from the office, and he'd say something like "hope you got your beauty sleep" or "no more working the graveyard shift," and that would be it. But he's not there and for a second you wonder if it's not Tuesday morning on a B day after all.

"Chase." Over by the leg press, with his square jaw, track pants, and Midlands High Cougars sweatshirt, the gym teacher waves you over with a sharp flick of his green clipboard.

You didn't know who he was when he walked into the main office moments before you were sentenced for stealing Jake the Jock's wallet, and even after he gave you that look that said that, for some god-knows-why reason, he believed you, you didn't think he knew your name.

But he knows it now.

"Pass." He holds out his hand, snapping his fingers. You hand him the crumpled paper. He keeps his eyes locked on yours as he unfolds it, then looks at the pass as if it were a counterfeit twenty you were trying to palm off as the real thing. He looks up at you, then back at the pass, before initialing the corner and securing it on the clipboard. "Well?" he says, and there is nothing friendly in his voice. You don't know what he wants you to say, so of course you say nothing.

There's something about the way he looks at you.

Something familiar.

Not annoyed.

Disgusted.

You expect it from your father—he's had fifteen years to build up to it.

But from a teacher? A teacher you don't even know? For being ten minutes late to class, with a valid excuse?

You turn and walk over to the incline bench press. You can feel his eyes burning into the back of your skull and part of you wants to turn around and say something. The other part just wants to keep walking.

This is everything that's in your locker at 10:42 a.m.:

- a biology textbook, stuffed with folded papers, some for that class
- a math textbook, similarly stuffed
- two identical history textbooks, one yours, one you found and thought was yours, both following the books-stuffed-with-papers pattern
- a French-English dictionary, which is strange since you're taking Spanish
- five notebooks, originally designated for separate classes, all now used arbitrarily based on which one you grabbed before class
- a paperback copy of *The Crucible*

- one sneaker, no laces
- a dead pay-as-you-go cell phone
- four empty Mountain Dew plastic bottles, one empty Red Bull can
- a black hooded sweatshirt with a red and white Independent Truck Company logo
- the CliffsNotes for *Romeo and Juliet*, new, never opened
- various empty candy wrappers
- an unlabeled CD, no case
- a key to the back door of your house you assumed was lost
- three pens, one of which works
- a first-quarter progress report, unopened, addressed to your parents
- seventy-three cents in change
- no drugs, alcohol, weapons, or other items deemed contraband

You know this because the vice principal made you stand there and watch as the security guards went through your locker during a "random" locker search.

Out of the fifteen hundred or so lockers at Midlands High School, yours was the only locker randomly selected.

At least they found that key.

The second quarter of the school year is only four weeks old, meaning there are still six weeks of school until the end of the first semester. That's thirty class days, give or take, with Christmas vacation in the middle of it. A lot of things can happen in six weeks, but apparently not you passing American History.

"Do the math and you'll get your answer," Mr. Bundinger says, tapping his finger on a row of zeros.

This from the man who doesn't know who the president of India is, who doesn't know that half the class is cheating on his quizzes, who thinks no one knows he uses the same tests every year, who thinks teaching is showing videos every class.

You suggest doing an extra-credit project, not because you would but because that's what you're expected to say and because you know what he'll say, and he does, pointing out how that wouldn't be fair to the other students or fair to you. You could point out that it's not fair that he lets the jocks turn in extra-credit projects to save their grades, and you don't mind if it's not fair to you, since he hasn't been fair to you since day one, but you know what he'd say to that and, in the end, like everything else, does it really make a difference?

"Kyle, what am I always saying in class? Those who don't learn from the past are doomed to repeat it."

You don't remember him ever saying anything like it, but this isn't the time to bring it up.

"What's true for history is true for history *class*."

He chuckles at his own joke. You don't think it's all that funny.

"Now, Kyle, I still expect you to hand in all the homework this quarter."

"Will I pass?"

"Right now you have a thirty-four-point-six percent average in this class. You could *possibly* move that up to fifty, fifty-five percent, if you worked at it."

"But will I pass?"

"Passing is a sixty-five."

So you do the math.

And the answer is you won't be doing any more American History this semester.

As soon as you see the guy at Sears, you know you didn't get the job.

He's got that uncomfortable look on his face that

all adults get when they're about to tell you that something's wrong. Not wrong with you—that look they have no problem with. Eyebrows arched up, eyes wide, mouth closed but chin still hanging, lower lip pushed out a bit. It's that I-know-I-let-you-down face, and even though you don't see it often, you recognize it. The bags under his eyes and his droopy cheeks only make it worse. But you went all the way home to put on this stupid outfit and walked all the way back to the mall, so you figure you might as well go through with it. You keep walking up to him and when you're still ten feet away he sticks his hand out.

"Uh, yeah. Kyle, right?" He grips your hand and starts shaking, a slow-motion version of yesterday's handshake. He looks around and then gives a nod at an empty register over in the men's department. "Let's step over here a second."

So you step over there for a second. He leans against the counter and buries his hands in his pants pockets. "How was school today?"

And you're thinking, just get it over with, but you mumble something about it being okay when it was anything but okay, but neither of you really care.

He sighs and shakes his head. "Kyle, I'm afraid I have some bad news."

Bad news? That you don't get to waste hours of your free time in a store you don't even like doing crap work for minimum wage?

"When we talked yesterday . . . I guess I left you with the impression that, uh . . . well, as it turns out there was a, um, another candidate for the job." He waves his hand as if he's still not sure where this second candidate popped up from himself. "The uh, the gist of it is that we decided to go with this . . . um . . . *other* applicant."

He pauses, waiting for you to jump in and make this easy for him, but you don't, and he waits a second longer before he starts in again, telling you that there are openings all the time, maybe none now, sure, but by late spring or summer, and that he'll keep your application at the top of the pile, let the other associate managers know to give you a call, and best of luck to you, Kyle, happy holidays.

A second, brief handshake and he's off to some back office and you're walking out into the mall.

You didn't want to apply for the job in the first place.

And you didn't want to go in for the interview.

Because you didn't really think they were going to hire you anyway.

So you were right.

So you should feel pretty good.

So?

Why don't you?

You knew the second message was going to be from Zack, but you scrolled down to it anyway.

"Greetings, young Chase, Zack McDade here.

As you no doubt observed, I was not among those present at Midlands High today, a fact that must have cast a dark shadow over the entire proceedings. But, with my parental unit out of town, I had the fortunate opportunity to entertain a rather eager and adventurous young lady at my home. It's amazing what some people will do if you just ask nicely. I even managed to get you a souvenir. Anyway, full details when we speak in person. Shall we say good old Midlands at nine tonight? I'll leave the window open for you. Till then, *au revoir, mon ami.*"

You delete the message, then look at the clock on your father's nightstand, the one above the drawer where you found your cell phone. Four forty. Your mom would be home first, picking Paige up from her after-school program on her way from work. Your father would roll in closer to six. You want to be gone before they get here. You won't be able to get into the school until after the maintenance crews have left, probably no earlier than nine. Over four hours to go, and already your jaw muscles ache from gritting your teeth. It'll be late for a school night and your parents will be pissed, but Zack will be at the school and there's no way you're not going to be there.

In your room, you take off the polo shirt you wore to the mall and fling it in the direction of your bed. You miss and it lands on the floor, followed by the jeans you were wearing. You pull on a black Warped Tour T-shirt and a pair of black jeans, yanking a black hoodie from your closet. Later, much will be made about the clothes you're wearing, but the truth is that you just grabbed what was there.

Back down the hall to your parents' room. You're not going to leave a note—that will be discussed tomorrow as well—but decide you'd better put your phone back where you found it. Not getting the job and staying out late are bad enough, no need to make it worse. Before you put it in the drawer, you look at the phone. You look at it for a full minute before you play the first message—the message Ashley sent last night—one more time.

"Kyle, oh my god, I really need to talk to you. *Ugh*, I didn't want to tell you in a voice mail, but I can't wait, I'm so excited. Okay, I'll just say it. I *really* love you."

If only the phone message ended right there.

It would be perfect and nothing else would matter, not your parents or school or the job thing.

Perfect.

But, just like the other eight times you played it, there's more.

And knowing what's coming doesn't make it any easier.

"You're like my best friend in the world, so I know you'll be happy for me, and not like all judgmental. Okay, you can't tell *anybody*, but guess who asked me to skip school with him tomorrow?"

The building is dark and you didn't see any cars in the parking lot, but you hang back along the trees for ten minutes, watching, just to be sure. You cut across the field, sticking to the shadows, angling in toward Zack's French class window.

By the time you get to the window the sweat's beading up on your forehead. It's not a nervous sweat because you're not nervous. And you don't sweat when you get angry, so it's not that. Then again, you've never been this angry before. If you thought about it you'd realize that it's an unusually warm night and you're wearing a hoodie. But you've got other things on your mind, don't you?

From outside, the window looks locked, but it slides open like it did the last time, and you slip inside as easy as an Xbox ninja. There's light coming through the window in the door, not much but enough to let you see your way around the room. You reach for the doorknob and stop.

The last time you pulled the door open the

alarm went off. If Zack is not here yet, if he hasn't punched in the code, the alarm will go off again.

What was the code?

Four numbers and the star key.

But which four?

You stand there for several minutes, replaying the scene in your head, Zack showing off and you ready to hit him.

What if you did? What if you had hauled off and smacked him one, right in his smart-ass mouth? Maybe that would have done it. It might have ended right there and you wouldn't have to be here now. But you didn't. You stood there and took it. He played you and you let him get away with it.

Those who don't learn from the past are doomed to repeat it.

You won't make that mistake again.

Eight, six, zero, four. The last four digits of the school's phone number. You open the door and step into the hallway.

No alarm.

And no Zack.

You start down the hallway, keeping close to the lockers. The alarm could be off because the cleaning crew is behind schedule or some ridiculously dedicated teacher is working late. You ease your way through the building, listening for voices and footsteps. The hum of faulty fluorescent lights, too low to hear during the day, masks any noise you might make, the same way they might mask the sound of someone creeping up behind you.

There's a cavernous black space behind the glass doors to the cafeteria. You know what's in there—a lot of metal picnic tables, the kind that they can fold in half and roll away, the aluminum racks where you're supposed to put the trays, not enough garbage cans. You don't check the doors to see if they're locked. Zack isn't in there. It's too dark and he likes the spotlight.

As if on cue, you hear the electric pop of the PA

system, the light tapping of a finger on the metal microphone, and then Zack's voice echoes down the corridors.

"Kyle Chase, please report to the main office."

He knows you're here—or he's guessing. And if there was anyone else in the building, they know now too. But you know it's just you and Zack. You can feel it. It's better this way.

You continue down the hall and make a turn. You go past the science labs, past the upper-level math classes, past the stairwell where you and Jake the Jock first met, past the office where the school psychologist asked you about your scar, and make the last turn to the main hall.

Zack is waiting for you by the trophy case. He's wearing his black sport coat and a bone-white shirt, a pair of those out-of-style jeans. He stretches his arms out wide, that smirk big on his face.

"Mr. Chase. *Outstanding*, sir, simply outstanding."

So far it's going pretty much the way you thought

it would. In the hours you wandered around the mall, waiting for nine to arrive, you thought through how you'd handle this. If you rushed him, he'd see it coming. He's not much bigger than you, but no reason to make it easy for him. And if you walked up with that look on your face, he'd see that, too. No, you have to do this differently.

Zack doesn't know what you know—and he's dying to tell you. That's why he called you here.

He finds your weak spot, then keeps pushing till you crack.

You didn't think you had any, but it turns out, you've got more than you thought. And he's found them all. But you're not going to crack. And he won't see it coming.

You step out of the shadow of the hallway and into the bright foyer by the trophy case, hands in your pockets, feet scuffing on the polished tile, smiling your best smile.

"Sorry I'm late. Couldn't get my locker open."

He gives a fake little laugh. It's the same laugh he's always used, only now it's lost its magic. "I hear a tire iron works nicely. How are you doing, sir?" He reaches his hand out and you shake it, the same old-fashioned way you shook the hand of the guy at Sears.

"Any problems getting in here?"

"*Moi?*" He steps back, acting hurt and surprised. "My good man, you offend me."

You shrug, playing it cool. "Hey, how am I supposed to know? You had a busy day, you might have been distracted."

He looks at you and there's this glint in his eye, and you know you said too much, too soon. He leans against the edge of the glass case, crosses his ankles then crosses his arms. Mr. Casual. "Indeed. It's been a *very* busy day."

"Really?" You put one hand up to the top of the trophy case, the other you keep in your pocket. It's not comfortable, but you hold the pose.

"Oh yeah, busy. Let's see, it started at ten this morning. I had an appointment with Mr. Loman. You know Mr. Loman, don't you?"

You shake your head.

"Sure you do. He's the assistant manager over at Sears. Great guy. See, last evening a little bird told me that you had gone in for a job interview, and I said to myself, Zack, you should see what you can do to help out your pal. So this morning I spruced myself up and went to see the man himself. We chatted for about an hour—your name came up, by the way—and in the end it turns out I'm *exactly* the kind of applicant he's looking for. Imagine that."

If he thought this would piss you off, he miscalculated. You look up to the ceiling as if you're trying to remember if you've ever been in a Sears before. He's watching you, you can feel it. He wants a reaction from you, wants to know he's found a way in. But you give him nothing.

"Oh, and I almost forgot," he continues. "Yesterday I had that little heart-to-heart with the lacrosse team coach, Mr. Comeau. You would have liked this, Chase. We're sitting in his office and I'm all teary-eyed, recounting how I was afraid that my only friend at venerable Midlands High was selling drugs—"

"You told him I sell drugs?" You feel your cheeks grow red, the muscles along your jaw start to burn, and you remember the way the man glared at you when he spit out your name.

"Oh, I can't remember who said what, but hints were dropped and names were named—or more specifically—*your* name was named. You see, I knew I wouldn't be there today and I didn't want you to get too bored. I thought a little police action would liven up your day."

"You set me up?"

"Mr. Chase, you make it sound so mean. It was meant as a fun little distraction, a break in your otherwise mundane routine. I thought you'd enjoy it."

"*Enjoy it?* Now that coach thinks I'm selling drugs."

"Since when did *you* care what Coach Comeau thought?"

You shouldn't care, really.

He's a coach, you're a hoodie.

But you do care. And you don't know why.

"What if I *had* something in my locker, huh? Then what?"

Zack shakes his head. "I checked. A few notebooks, a dead phone, a ridiculous sweatshirt, sort of like the one you're wearing. No, nothing *verboten*, Chase. However . . ." He drags the word out, enjoying the effect the word has on you, your teeth clenched now and eyes narrowing. "However," he says again, "I *sure* hope they don't check your gym locker *too* early in the morning."

You want to run to the locker room, but you know

that that's what he wants you to do. He even inclines his head down the back hall that leads to the gym, tempting you to go. But you don't. Whatever it is—if it's anything at all—it'll be there when you're done. Instead, you ask him the obvious question.

"Why are you doing this to me?"

"To *you*?" Zack's eyes widen in surprise. "What makes you think *you're* so special? This is what I do with *everyone*, Chase. I'm sure someone must have told you that."

"But why?"

"Why do *you* do what you do, Mr. Chase?" He uncrosses his arms to give an elaborate shrug, stepping away from the trophy case. "Why do any of us do the stupid things we do? Why does Nicole spread her legs as soon as someone tells her she's pretty? Why does Josh pay me money to come to my parties? Why does my mother leave me alone for days *knowing* the kind of things I get up to? Why does Brooke come crawling back every time I throw her away, or Victoria buy me things I don't ask for? And you, young Mr. Chase." He stops and faces you, dropping his arms. "Why do you hang around with me?"

You didn't expect the question. And you certainly don't have an answer. If you did, you wouldn't be here.

Zack takes a short step closer. "This is who we are, who we let ourselves be. All of us, playing roles. All the world's a stage, remember? All the men and women merely players. Some are sluts, some are fools, some are bullies, and some—the very few—the truly bold—they get the spotlight."

"And *you're* the star?" And now you laugh.

"Oh, I get a few good lines now and then, but I'm more of a director. It's much more interesting."

"So you screw with people's lives just for the fun of it?"

"Don't blame me, Mr. Chase." He takes another step closer. Almost close enough. "I never told you what to do, I never tell anyone what to do. I make suggestions, I provide opportunities, and I make them *very* tempting, but when it comes down to it, everyone makes their own bad decisions. Now is it *my* fault that what they choose to do is exactly what I want them to do?"

If your head were clear, if you were thinking straight, you'd know it was true. It's always been true. Your whole life is a chain of choices—your choices. It was your choices that landed you in Midlands in the first place. You could have chosen to stay tight with the friends you had instead of hanging around with losers, but that was another choice you made. And as far as grades, nobody forced you to become the kind of student who has few choices left.

If you thought about it you'd realize that you don't have control over everything, but you control how you react. You couldn't choose the way your father treats you, but he didn't make you punch a hole in the wall. And who forced you to trash the men's room at the mall, or sucker punch that kid last year, or smash your alarm clock, or the thousand other stupid things you've done?

How You Got That Scar on the Back of Your Hand, Part 4. The Truth. You chose to put it there.

And Ashley? You couldn't make her like you, that's her choice. But you chose not to even try.

If you were thinking clearly, all of these things would make sense, but you're not, so the only thing that makes sense is going on with your plan. He's closer now, but you're careful not to tense up. Not yet.

"So you see, I don't screw up other people's lives, Mr. Chase. They are quite eager to do it themselves. And speaking of screwing . . ." He lets his words trail off, knowing he's got you now.

You lower your arm from the top of the trophy case—slow, relaxed—and hook your thumb on the saggy edge of your jeans. You shift the weight, balance yourself. Still, not yet.

"Ashley told me you guys were skipping school today," you say, trying to steal the moment from him. And you say it so easy, like it's some other girl and some other guy, not Ashley and Zack. "Have a good time?"

He's surprised, his smirk dipping, but he recovers and the smirk returns, bigger than before. "Yes, Mr. Chase, we *did* have a good time. Ashley is quite a wild woman, you know, up for everything I suggested. Made a few suggestions of her own, too. Very talented. Well, you'd almost expect it with that tight little body, don't you think? Believe me, it's as good as you've imagined."

Your jaw tightens, you can't control it. You feel your breathing change, your heart rate pick up steam.

"She mentioned you as well. Oh, not in the middle of anything. After. Well, after the second time."

"What did she say?" Your voice surprises you.

You weren't going to say a thing.

"You confused her, Mr. Chase." Zack takes a half step closer. "She couldn't understand why you never asked her out. All those months, all those phone calls. Don't worry, I cleared it all up for her, told her how you were questioning your sexuality and how you thought she was flat and unattractive but still a good friend. Yeah, you're all set now. And don't worry about me, I'm done with her. Too easy."

Your fingers curl into fists and you feel your arms drawing back. Zack sees it, too, but he still stands there, hands on his hips.

"Wait just a moment," he says in a voice that's part soothing, part assertive. "I brought a peace offering." Slowly he lifts one hand, raising his index finger, turning his wrist to point into the trophy case. "Got it special for you, Kyle. A little *souvenir*."

You keep your eyes on him but turn your head, then give a quick glance in the case. It's deep— three feet at least—with raised platforms and

Roman column pedestals all supporting decades'
worth of trophies. Tarnished metal quarterbacks
in midthrow; skirted tennis players knocking fierce
backhands; wrestlers ready for you to make a move;
centers rolling in the layup; newer plastic versions
with similar poses; trophies topped with miniature
baseballs, lacrosse sticks, and soccer balls; lowly par-
ticipation awards alongside division championships;
wood plaques with rows of brass nameplates next to
signed game balls and squads of formal team photos.

And along the back wall of the case, taller, shinier
than the rest, isolated, impossible to miss, a multi-
tiered state championship trophy, a golden athlete
with his arms raised in victory.

In one hand he holds a wreath, and from the
other dangles a bright red lace thong.

Tied at the crotch, a white tag with a computer-
printed label.

PROPERTY OF ASHLEY BIANCHI.

You feel your breath catch and your stomach

cramp, your knees threaten to buckle, and you see your reflection sway. And you can picture Ashley, pushing through the crowd of students Zack will have summoned, seeing what you see, seeing what everybody will see, Zack cracking her with his first push.

Behind you, you can hear Zack laughing.

There's only one thing to do, so you do it.

Now.

Fist up, arm cocked back shoulder level, hips one way, then snap the other, your whole body falling forward into the punch.

Everything in this one punch.

Anger.

Frustration.

Fear.

Hate.

Love.

With a frightening crash, the glass shatters, buckling in large sheets that collapse into the case, knocking over trophies and shredding championship banners. The punch propels you into the case, your foot bracing against the frame. Glass falls around you, but you keep leaning in until, with one last lunge, you grab the thong, yanking it free. To the victor go the spoils.

You always knew it would be different with Ashley. And it still could be.

For months, you chose to do nothing. But now you choose to act, and things will be different. You'll tell her the things you always wanted to tell her, the things you know she wants to hear. Because with you, things will be different. And you'll never tell her about what Zack said, and you'll make damn sure he doesn't tell anyone else.

It's going to be different now, you can feel it.

And that's when you notice the blood.

Your arm sliced open from wrist to armpit, that final lunge shoving the pointed shard deep inside, holding you up.

You're surprised at all the blood.

He looks over at you, eyes wide, mouth dropping open, his face almost as white as his shirt.

He's surprised, too.

There's not a lot of broken glass, though, just some tiny slivers around his feet and one big piece, busted into sharp peaks like a spiking line graph, the blood washing down it like rain on a windshield.

He doesn't say anything clever or funny, doesn't quote Shakespeare, he just screams. But no one can hear him, and it would be too late if they could.

You're thinking, this wasn't the way it was supposed to go, this shouldn't be happening. And now things are only going to get worse.

You're just a kid.

It can't be your fault.

But then there's all that blood.

So, maybe it is your fault, but it doesn't make it any better.

And it doesn't matter one way or the other.

Think.

When did it go wrong?

The break-in?

No, before that.

The party?

That was part of it, but that wasn't when it started.

Zack?

Of course, yeah, it would be easy to say it was Zack. But that's not it, is it?

Before Zack.

Before Ryan. Before Max or Derrick or that whole thing with the wallet.

Before Ashley.

Before tenth grade even began.

And you're thinking, this can't be it.

FALL
FROM
GRACE

CHAPTER

"**I NEED YOU** to steal something for me."

She was small, with dark hair and blue eyes that looked lit from behind, and the kind of face, the kind of tight body that kept him listening.

"Get me a copy of the treaty you're working on. The one with Iran."

He shrugged. "I don't know what you're talking about."

"Don't play dumb. I saw you sitting with the delegation at the opening ceremony. North Korea, right?"

"Yeah." A pause, another shrug. "I think so."

"You *think* so? You don't know what country you're with?"

1

"I just joined Thursday."

"Is that your school's team?" She pointed across the gym to the folding table where a kid in a suit and two girls in dresses huddled around one of the laptops. The table was centered under a MODEL UNITED NATIONS banner taped to the backboard above the basketball hoop.

"It's the team I'm with, yeah."

"Then you're North Korea. So you can get it for me."

He smiled. He had to. There was something about her that made him do it. "Who are you?"

"Grace." She pulled on the name tag clipped to an empty belt loop of her red jeans.

"I meant the country you're with."

"Belgium." She tapped the black, yellow, and red flag printed on the school team ID as if the answer was obvious. West High School. A Westie. The other side of the proverbial tracks. The wrong side. "Where's *your* ID, comrade?"

He patted his chest, then checked his pockets. "I must have lost it."

"Tsk-tsk. Now you won't get to enjoy a delicious cafeteria-style box lunch." She looked at him, her head tilted to the side a bit, her hair bouncing short of her shoulder. "So maybe you're smarter than you look."

"It's the tie. I had to wear one."

She reached up and gave it a tug. "At least it's not a

clip-on." It wasn't, but it might as well have been. His father had tied it for him months ago and each time he wore it, he slipped it off over his head, hanging it on the hook on the back of his bedroom door, the misshapen knot pulled too tight to untangle. "So, you gonna get me that treaty?"

"What do you need it for?"

"Do you really care?"

"I might."

"You don't. It's a make-believe treaty written by a bunch of high school students pretending to be the ambassadors of real countries they couldn't find on a map. Picking a theme for the senior prom has more global impact."

That wasn't the way Mr. Jansen had explained Model United Nations, but so far it was the most accurate description he'd heard. He had joined late in the quarter, too late to know what he was supposed to be doing, but, as his mother had pointed out, not too late to add it to his college application. She said he needed an extracurricular activity, something academic, that he could list along with all the volunteer work his parents had arranged for him to do. His father would have preferred that he join Public Speaking, but that would have meant speaking in public, and as determined as they were on getting him into a good school, even his parents couldn't get around that. That's why they settled on MUN. He was just glad they didn't know there was a chess club.

"I've been to this school before," Grace said, looking past the open gym doors and down the long corridor. "There's a photocopier in the teachers' lounge. I'll have it back in five minutes, tops."

"If you think this whole thing is stupid—"

"And I do, but go on."

"—why do you want the treaty?"

"*I* don't want it, the US team wants it. I'm cutting a little deal on the side. I get them the details of the treaty, they give me North Dakota."

"Why would you want North Dakota?"

"It would complete the set. Look, you going to get it for me or not?"

"If I don't, what happens then?"

"Then we both have to think of something to do to fill up the four hours before this ridiculous event is over."

He could think of plenty of things they could do for four hours, and if he were that kind of guy, the put-it-out-there kind who was smooth with the words and fast with the ladies, they'd be off in some empty classroom, getting busy. He wasn't, not even close, but that didn't stop him from thinking about it. Besides, Zoë would find out for sure and she'd be pissed and she'd tell his mother because they were tight like that and then he'd hear

4

about it from his parents, plus he'd have to see Zoë—and all of Zoë's friends—every day in school, and he could guess what that would be like. Nope, even if he was that kind of guy it wasn't worth it. Still, for an uncontrolled, hormone-driven second, he thought about it.

"Four hours at a MUN event is a long, long time," she said. "If you don't help get the treaty I'll be so bored I'll probably declare war on Luxembourg and then you'll have that on your conscience."

He weighed the pretend global consequences before nodding. "Anything for world peace. Wait here, I'll go get it."

"Hold it." She grabbed his wrist and pulled him back, stronger than she looked. Her hand was cool and dry against his skin. "You just can't walk up and take it."

"Yes I can. There're copies on the table, I'll get one and—"

"We have to have a plan first. And signals and code words and a Plan B and an escape route. . . ."

"How about this for a plan? I go get it and give it to you."

"Oh, come on. You're taking all the fun out of it."

"You *are* bored. Okay, what's the plan?"

The metal bleachers were pushed closed against the wall, but someone had pulled out a couple rows at the bottom where delegates from around the make-believe world had tossed their book bags and winter coats. She led him to an open section and took a seat, flipping to a blank page in a notebook that wasn't hers.

"We'll call it Operation Trick-or-Treat."

"Because you like Halloween?"

"No, because I like taking candy from babies." She wrote the words at the top of the paper in blocky capital letters. She drew a quick map of the gym and the hallway. "Next, we need code names. I'll be Al'ea and you can be Bix."

"Bix? What kind of name is Bix?"

She looked at him, stunned by his ignorance. "Al'ea and Bix? From *Reality Frat House?*"

Blank stare.

"You're kidding, right? They're *famous*."

"Famous for what?"

"For being famous, geez, what do you think? They're on TV, that's all they have to do." She shook her head and mumbled as she continued to map out the room. "I can't believe you don't know who Bix is."

"How about calling me Sawyer?"

"Which Sawyer? The one from *Random Roommates* or the one from *Spring Break Survival*?"

"The one from East High School."

"That's your name? Sawyer?" She gave him the quick up and down. "No, it doesn't fit. Let's go with Bix. But just for this job."

"Good. It would be a pain to have to get my driver's license changed."

She focused on the paper, drawing arrows one way, erasing them and going another, the tip of her tongue sticking out between her lips as she made the simple complex. He leaned forward, elbows on his knees, and waited. Nothing else to do. The North Korean team— his team—were bent over their laptops, finalizing the resolutions he wasn't allowed to help with. Well, he *could* if he *really* wanted to, but it's just that it's so *late* in the process and the team had already *done* all the background work and he'd have *so far* to go to catch up and he could still play an important role, sure, but not with the writing or the presenting or the debates, definitely not the debates, but sorta like a goodwill ambassador, that way he could get to know how the event works so next time he can play a bigger role—well not *next* time, since that's the regionals, but after that, maybe. They were sure he understood.

"All right, we're here," Grace said, tapping two small Xs with the point of her pencil. "Here's North Korea, and right next to it is Denmark. I'll go to the Denmark table, and I'll make something up about how they should join Belgium in blocking imports from countries with dictatorships. That'll get your team all hot and bothered.

Meanwhile, you come around like this, between Kuwait and Kyrgyzstan. Wait by Trinidad. When you hear me say 'Why do you think they call them *dic*tators,' you grab the paper, then make your way over to Singapore and leave the paper behind those blue mats. I'll head to Mexico. Give me the sign when you've planted the paper and I'll go pick it up."

"What sign is that?"

"Ever see *The Sting*?" She held up a finger and tapped it along the side of her nose.

"Another reality show?"

"You don't know *The Sting*? What do they teach you over at East?" She shook her head some more. "I'll pick up the paper, take it down to the teachers' lounge, and burn a copy. It would be easier to just take a picture of it, but the US team has crappy phones so they need a hard copy. I'll put the original back by the mats, then you put it back in the folder. Easy." She folded the paper and stuck it in her jeans, dropping the pencil in the pocket of his shirt. "Now, you ready for this?"

CHAPTER

AS SOON AS he opened his locker, Sawyer knew someone had gone through it.

Things had been rearranged, not a lot but enough to
notice—notebooks that he always kept on the floor were
on the shelf, the paperbacks were lined up by size, his spare
hoodie moved from the right hook to the left, the magnetic
mirror moved halfway down the inside of the door.

The first person that came to mind was Zoë.

Two years ago, before they started enforcing the no-
sharing-lockers rule, she had used his locker as a dumping
ground for the things she didn't want to carry or as over-
flow storage when her locker was too trashed to cram in
any more. But that all changed after the knife incident
at West High, and now the administration viewed using
someone else's locker as a Homeland Security violation.
Besides, his locker wasn't anywhere near Zoë's classes
and she had enough trouble remembering her own

9

combination, let alone his. And if for some reason she *had* gone through his locker, she would never have left it so neat.

There was always the chance that it had been the security guards looking for drugs. They'd never checked lockers before, but that didn't mean they couldn't start. Not that they would have found anything—not that they'd even think of him as the type of kid to bring drugs to school—but as he tried to figure out who'd been in his locker, the security guards were an option.

Then he saw the paper bag in the back corner. It was the same size bag you'd get if you bought a liter of Mountain Dew, and even with the top of the bag scrunched closed, he knew there was a bottle inside. He also knew he hadn't put it there.

Sawyer knelt down and moved in closer. He made a show of moving some books around, flipping through binders for a paper he was wasn't looking for, and when there was a lull in traffic, he reached into the top of the bag and felt the pointed teeth of a bottle cap.

Someone had left him a beer.

If Dillon had been in town and if they were still close, Sawyer would have assumed it was him. But since Dillon wasn't in town and they weren't close, Sawyer kept thinking. If he felt the tapered neck of a wine cooler or the smooth metal sides of a Bacardi O twist-off, he would have thought Zoë. But it was beer, and beer wasn't Zoë. It could have been a setup, the kind of prank assholes did to get somebody suspended, putting alcohol into someone's locker and tipping off the administration. He'd never heard of it happening at East, but he could be the first.

Crouched in tight, Sawyer inched the dark brown bottle from the bag.

Duvel Belgian golden ale.

Taped to the back of the bottle was a note:

WELL DONE, 007.
CHEERS,
G

Sawyer moved quick, putting the bottle back in the bag, laying the bag on its side, then stacking books around it to keep it hidden.

It would be hours before he'd have a chance to sneak it into his backpack and out of the school, and he knew he'd be sweating the entire time. He never did anything wrong, and it would be just his luck to get busted the very first time. What the hell was this girl Grace thinking? And how'd she get in his locker in the first place, or even known where his locker was? And what was she doing at East?

He moved the mirror back in place, and when he saw

himself smiling he had to admit that, okay, okay, it *was* funny.

Stupid funny.

Just like at the MUN event.

She was right, he had been bored and he hadn't cared about the treaty and helping her steal it did make the day go by faster. It was stupid and immature and uncalled for and disrespectful and all that.

But it was fun.

His parents wouldn't think so, and Zoë would've gone ballistic if she knew he had spent the day conspiring with a Westie girl no matter *how* they met, but his parents didn't have to know and maybe he didn't have to tell Zoë everything.

As he closed his locker and headed to English class— late for the first time all year—Sawyer wondered what else Grace did for fun.

CHAPTER

TWO WEEKS LATER, there she was again.

He was working the Sunday afternoon shift at Mike's Ice Cream, and if it were summer or if the sun had been out, it would have been busy, but nobody thinks *ice cream* when it's cold and wet and gray. Five, six customers since the shift started and there'd be maybe that many more before it was over. For the hundredth time he wiped down the spotless counter and tried to tune out the satellite radio permanently set to the '50s channel.

His father was in the same golf league as the owner, which is why Sawyer got the job and why he had to keep it. There were times, though, more now that the weather was crap and the four hours felt like four hundred, when he wondered what it would be like to quit and find a job on his own, something he actually enjoyed doing or that was at least a challenge. Then he'd think about what his parents would say and that would be the end of that.

He had finished with the counter and had moved on to the metal sink by the register where they kept the ice cream scoops when the reindeer bells on the back of the door rang and she walked in. The combat boots, the bright purple jacket zippered up tight against the red scarf, the two white wires leading out from under the black knit cap, that was all different, but the way he was pulled in by her eyes was the same.

He rearranged the scoops in the sink, careful not to let her catch him looking. He knew she knew, but that's the game and how it's played. And she played her part. He watched her reflection in the cooler window as she stuffed the hat in her pocket and pushed her hair behind her ears. An earbud dropped free and she left it dangling as she walked to the counter. He looked up and gave her the do-I-know-this-girl head tilt, followed by a hey-it's-you-again smile, trying to act like he wasn't acting.

She smiled too, with him or at him, he wasn't sure.

"The ice cream man," she said, leaning up against the counter. "Are all your flavors guaranteed to satisfy?"

"Except for the no-fat ones. Nobody likes those." He dropped a stray spoon in the sink and wiped his hands on his Mike's Ice Cream apron. "What brings you way over here?"

She took a step back and put up her hands in mock surprise. "Sorry, sheriff. Didn't know us no-account

Westsiders weren't welcome in these here east parts."

"It's lousy out there," Sawyer said, pointing his chin toward the gray windows. "Far to go just for ice cream."

"I didn't come all this way for the ice cream," she said, looking at him as she said it, pausing as she leaned back in. "I came for the library."

"They've got one on the west side. By the Kmart."

"This one's twice the size and it's got a better law section." She looked past him to the board that listed forty-six flavors even though they didn't carry half that many. He watched those blue eyes dart along the rows of the names and watched her lips twitch as she read. He gave her time to work her way through them all, then said, "What do you want me to make you?"

"Famous. But for now just give me a small chocolate espresso ripple."

He wrapped a white napkin around the cone, then flipped open the curved glass case and scooped up a large serving. Bent over the tubs of ice cream, he could hear the tinny bass of her dangling earbud as she pressed against the glass. He offered sprinkles, she said no, she tried to give him a five but he wouldn't take it, telling her he was allowed to give away one free cone a day and she was it, a lie that worked for the both of them.

She tasted the ice cream. She could have done some long, slow lick thing, her tongue curling around the base of the scoop and working up slowly, *real* slowly, to the tip, all the while peeking out from under half-closed, smoky lashes, like Zoë and her friends would do when they were messing with him, acting all slutty just to get a rise out of him. But she didn't. She licked the ice cream like normal and that was it.

"Rancid," she said, running the back of her hand across her lips.

"Oh, sorry. Here, let me give you a new one."

"Not the ice cream. The band. It's Rancid. I saw your hand going with the beat, figured you'd want to know."

He didn't, but was impressed she had noticed one finger that barely moved.

"This is yummy. Thanks."

"The law stuff at the library. Is it for school?"

She shook her head and took a bite out of her ice cream, taking her time before answering. "No, something for me. Looking for loopholes."

"You could have looked it up online."

"I could've, but then no ice cream."

The pause, the clever comeback—she was done talking about it and he knew that, but he couldn't stop himself. "Did you find what you were looking for?"

Another pause. "Maybe. I'll let you know."

There was nothing left to talk about but he was in no hurry to see her go. Then he remembered his locker and said, "Oh yeah. Thanks for the beer."

"Thanks for North Dakota."

"How'd you know which locker was mine?"

She was focused on her ice cream and he thought she didn't hear the question, but then she said, "You'd be surprised what you can find online these days. And how simple it is to guess the password for your school's database. Seriously, the mascot's name? Please."

He was impressed. "They have the combination on there too?"

"Didn't need it."

"How'd you get in?"

"Family secret," she said, and winked as she said it.

Across the shop the bells jingled as a pack of Cub Scouts burst in and raced to the counter, followed by a pair of mothers who repeated ignored warnings about not running and using inside voices and not touching anything, apologizing in advance for the trouble they knew they brought with them.

Somewhere between the double-scoop cookie dough cone and the raspberry sundae, he noticed that Grace was gone.

9 780061 947063